STARFISH

STARFISH

Patty Dann

GREENPOINT PRESS
NEW YORK, NY

ISBN 978-0-9886 968-2-2

Library of Congress Cataloging-in-Publication Data

Designed by Robert L. Lascaro, LascaroDesign.com
Type: cover title, chapter heads and drop caps set in Clarks Summit; proverbs
set in Helvetica Neue; text set in Century Schoolbook Expanded

Greenpoint Press,
a division of New York Writers Resources
greenpointpress.org
PO Box 2062
Lenox Hill Station
New York, NY 10021

New York Writers Resources:
· newyorkwritersresources.com
· newyorkwritersworkshop.com
· greenpointpress.org
· ducts.org

Printed in the United States
on acid-free paper

For Michael

IN 1212 A.D., thousands of children left their families to join what is now known as the Children's Crusade. Although it is said that they were followed by clouds of butterflies and schools of fish, nobody knows if any of these children ever made their way home.

1991

CHAPTER 1

"Adam ate the apple,
and our teeth still ache."

—Hungarian Proverb

When you hear of a fourteen-year-old girl in crazy love with a twenty-nine-year-old man, the next line you hear should include the word "shotgun," but the fact is, I was the girl, and I never loved anyone like I loved Joe Peretti. I thought of Joe saying "bell tower" in his New England accent every day for twenty-seven years, his voice like an oboe playing a perfect note, a voice that helped soothe my addled brain.

We moved to the house next door to the Protectors of the Blessed Souls Convent in Grove, Massachusetts in 1963, the house where Joe had lived with his family before his parents died and before he became caretaker at the convent. That convent was a refuge for Joe and

for me, clinging to each other for dear life. My sister
Kate almost drowned the night I was with Joe in the
bell tower. The last time I saw her was eleven years ago,
when she visited me in Eugene, Oregon and answered
the door for the UPS man with her shirt unbuttoned.
I haven't seen Joe since he fled town a few days after
our sin. When the incident happened, the only conse-
quence was small-town gossip. Now, I have moved back
to Grove at age forty-two.

Our family left Grove in 1964, at the end of the school
year, as we left many towns, twenty-two to be exact; and,
perhaps because of this, I've always found life to be as
fragile as an egg-and-spoon race on a sunlit lawn. When
I finally did graduate from high school, we happened to
be living in Eugene, Oregon, so I was able to go to the
university and pay in-state tuition. I got my masters in
English and stayed put, but Mrs. Flax and Kate had left
town years before. I always called my mother Mrs. Flax.
I last saw her eight years ago, when I visited her in San
Antonio, where I went for a teachers' work conference
while she was living there. She moved on soon afterwards, as she always did.

Carrie Giordano, who lives in Grove, became the
closest I ever had to a best friend, calling me every
week to talk on the phone after my family moved away.
You wouldn't be wrong if you called her a mother figure,
even though she was an Avon Lady and wore all the cosmetics she sold and size 6, form-fitting dresses. She sells
environmentally safe cosmetics and herbal teas now and

is still a perfect size 6, but wears one-size-fits-all muslin clothes and has let her hair go gray. Everyone in town calls Carrie's husband, Tim, "the tree guy," which means he's missing a couple of fingers. Tim might show up at your house to trim trees just as the sun is beginning to set, but he has a very good heart. In wintertime, he teaches drivers education at Grove High. Carrie and Tim have two daughters who grew up and moved away and one cockeyed son, Kenneth, who Carrie had when she was almost forty.

When our old house in Grove became available to rent, Carrie called me. Within a week, I jumped in my faded yellow Mazda and drove across America in five days, even though the convent was no longer there. Carrie also told me about the teaching job at the community college. I work there with people new to America, which I like, because I've always felt like a foreigner myself.

After my zigzag childhood, I take no pleasure in change. That's why I'd stayed in Eugene all those years. But Carrie knew that it was my dream to move back to Grove, to rethread my life, to get over my wild love for Joe. I figured if I could walk on the same hallowed ground, and even hallowed floors, where Joe and I had walked, it could be like an exorcism, and I would be catapulted into the future, or at least the present tense.

I never married, although I have a grown son, Nick. Nick's father, Bill, didn't stay around to meet his son. Nick lives in Rochester, New York, with his wife, Regina, who is twelve years older, and their twin toddler girls. Nick and Regina met at the University of Oregon. Kate is now thirty-three and still single like me. Kate once was content as long as she was swimming. She slept with her bathing suit on and always smelled of chlorine, but she lost interest in the sport when she developed breasts, at which point she became a wild girl.

When Kate was young, I liked to pretend she was my own child. She broke her arm when she fell out of a tree in Anniston, Alabama, and I got a special pass from my teacher so I could go to the cafeteria when she had lunch and help her eat. I was the one who wrapped and unwrapped her swim trophies each time we moved, dusting them off like they were sacred relics.

Kate went to nursing school, and she finds work in emergency rooms. Kate also makes a mean barbecue sauce. When Kate's around, I must batten down the hatches. Kate is by her nature a thunderstorm.

In an attempt to put my exploded family back together again, I decided to have a sixtieth birthday party for Mrs. Flax on Labor Day weekend in Grove. My hope was that both she and Kate would show up.

⁓

On Mondays, Thursdays and Fridays, I teach an English class at Grove Community College, and on the prickly hot July Monday after the Fourth, I dressed in as cool a cotton sleeveless dress as I could find. I am five feet two inches, with olive skin. I get highlights in my hair, which is for the most part still dark and curly.

I grabbed my book bag, went out the front door to the porch and noticed that the little metal door of the mailbox on the side of the house was open.

The year we lived in Grove, when I was fourteen, our mailbox was at the end of the driveway, not on the side of the house, like it is now. I would head down in our blue Buick station wagon and pick up Kate, with her wild curls bobbing, as she stood with her thumb out, pretending to be a hitchhiker.

"Hop in, kiddo," I'd say as I steered to the mailbox to check for mail. Sometimes we folded letters into hand-made envelopes and stamped them with S&H Green Stamps we filched from the kitchen drawer. We always put up the little red metal flag to show the mailman there was mail to collect. If we were really lucky, when we got to the mailbox, the nuns would be driving out in their se-rious black nun car, and I would put my face into a little smile and look as holy as I could. But today I reached my hand inside the mailbox on the side of the house and took out two supermarket flyers and a very thin enve-lope. It was one of those pale blue aerogrammes, folded neatly, with the letter as part of the envelope. It was light as air, so a plane full of them wouldn't tumble down into the sea.

I lifted it and pressed it to my nose. I thought I might smell sea air or perhaps perfume, but there was only the slight mildew scent of the inside of the mailbox.

On the envelope was my name, written in old-fashioned, slightly deranged-looking handwriting:

Miss or Mrs. Charlotte Flax

My address in Eugene was crossed out and, next to it, my current address was written in a scribbled hand:

4 Harvest Road

Grove, Massachusetts 01730

The return address, which did not include a name, was:

3 Woodsley Road

Leeds, LS29LZ

England

I usually rip open envelopes on the porch, but not this one. I knew that if I ripped the aerogramme I would tear the letter. The only people I'd ever gotten aerogrammes from before had been my grandparents, back when Mrs. Flax and my sister and I were always moving. When I was sixteen, I ran away while we were living near Chicago. It took me only a day to hitchhike to my grandparents, who had a kosher bakery in Minerva, Ohio. They let me stay, and I decided I wasn't moving again. I even went to classes on Kabbalah, and one night I chopped my hair short and for three months wore an old scratchy wig of my grandmother's as I tried to get back to my Jewish roots.

Now, years later, I held onto that envelope, wanting to will my grandparents back to life, wanting my grandfather to be taking a nap on the linoleum kitchen floor as the pear pies were baking, as if this were the way humans are supposed to be. Seven months after I moved in with my grandparents, my grandmother died of a stroke while she was making chocolate toffee squares. In those wild, numb days there is no name for, I fled home from school to do load after load of laundry for my grandfather and wash the last clothes my grandmother had worn before she died. Although it did not save my grandmother, it is what allowed me to survive. I've often thought in the years since her death of opening a Mourners' Cleaning Service.

I looked at the handwriting and return address again. Who'd be writing to me from England?

I decided it would have to wait. I stuffed the aerogramme into my school bag and drove off to the college in my slow-driving way, past the sugar maple trees in the town square tied with fraying yellow ribbons in honor of soldiers who had fought in the Gulf War. The war had officially ended in February, but there were still troops on the ground dealing with the oil fires in Kuwait.

The dean at the college had said we should think of the new American students as raisins in raisin bread rather than as ingredients in a melting pot. I ask them to bring in proverbs from their home countries, and I've started collecting these sayings in a spiral notebook I keep by my bed.

That day, I kept confusing and mispronouncing the names of the students. I always pride myself on getting the pronunciation right—the special "u" of Danish, the singsong intonation of Korean and the birdlike sound of Lithuanian. But, that day, I felt tone-deaf, fumbling along, trying to be sure to look directly at each of them. I believe a Romanian woman said her mother used to throw a rooster down the chimney to clean it out, but I can't be sure.

I help the students with their speech, on the theory that if their English were better, they wouldn't feel so excluded. Few of them know the word "excluded," however. A Chinese man said they feel "loop out," which I interpreted as "out of the loop." We were talking about the correct use of "his" and "her" when a Colombian man raised his hand and asked, "If the father drove her car, is the car a he or a she?"

When I turned to write the correct possessive for father on the chalkboard, I got tears in my eyes. For it was at that moment that I realized, although perhaps I had known it instantly, that the light blue aerogramme letter, written by someone who did not know if I was married or single or probably even alive, was from my father, whom I have no recollection of ever meeting and whose name I didn't even know. When Mrs. Flax spoke about him, which was almost never, she called him Mr. Flax, so I did, too. But Flax was her name. She wouldn't tell me his. For years, I had worn a pair of go-go boots that for no rational reason I had believed he sent to me.

A teacher should not be in tears in front of a classroom at the thought of receiving a letter from her father. This was not what I had planned. So I did what I rarely do. I stood facing the chalkboard, cleared my throat and said, "I will be back in a few moments" and scurried out of the room.

I made my blurry-eyed way to the ladies' room and

pushed open the door. There, I walked in on a fresh-faced student standing at the sink, poised to put in a contact lens.

I quickly turned on the water full blast in the second sink and washed my face.

"Allergies," I announced, as if this young woman cared. She stayed at the sink, holding her lens on the tip of her index finger, trying to insert it into her eye.

There were no towels, only those ridiculous blower machines, so I tried bending down to hold my face under the blower, wishing I were in an Oregon hot spring rather than a New England bathroom. Then I wiped my face with my sleeve as I hurried back into the hall.

When I returned to my classroom, my students were filing out, but a man stood at my desk, a man who looked like he would have no problems adapting to America or anywhere else, and he was holding a business card in his hand. He had a shock of blond hair and gray eyes and looked to be ten years younger than me. He was wearing a navy blue t-shirt, jeans and Nike running shoes. Looking at the card in his hand, I flushed when I had the sudden thought of kissing the inside of his wrists.

"Miss Charlotte," he said in an Eastern European accent. "I am Darius. I am inviting you to my home for having coffee on Wednesday morning at ten o'clock a.m. You will come?"

"Why, thank you, Darius. This is very kind of you," I said, almost imitating his accent, although I did not say yes or no.

"Here is my address," he said, and, as he handed me the card, he added, "I am waiting for you."

That afternoon, I drove home patting my school bag with the aerogramme in it and, now, Darius's business card, too.

—⌂—

CHAPTER 2

"God promises a safe landing
but not a calm passage."

—Bulgarian Proverb

When Mrs. Flax, my sister Kate and I lived in Grove
next door to the Protectors of the Blessed Souls
Convent, the nuns used to walk by in their black habits
and black, polished shoes, with their heads bent, chant-
ing into their Latin prayer books. I always thought they
were saying, "My mommy and daddy are in fifth grade,
my mommy and daddy are in fifth grade."

Nuns had begun to leave the convent even then, although I never saw one of them go. They could have
been stealing away in the darkest shadows of the night,
hurrying along the paths with their skirts lifted above
their ankles. It was rumored that one nun married a
pharmacist in Boston and their daughter now had the

fancy catering place in town.

When we lived in the house next door to the convent, Kate and I moved into Joe's old bedroom, the one with "Red Sox" carved into the door. That is now where I sleep. Mrs. Flax, who always put on red lipstick before she got out of bed in the morning, slept in Joe's parents' room. I use that as a guest room, although, so far, there have been no guests.

The convent, which housed thirty-seven nuns and one Mother Superior when we lived there, consisted of a handful of modest, slate gray buildings, a tiny chapel that reeked of incense, a stone bell tower with eighty-nine stone steps to the top, a pond, and even a basketball court. Mossy paths connected the buildings in an intricate labyrinth. Now, only the bell tower, where Joe Peretti and I did ungodly things, and the pond that caused so much drama, remain. The bell tower houses all the cable equipment for a condominium community called Colonial Gracious Homes, built on the convent's grounds. There is an Olympic-sized pool in place of the macadam court where the nuns used to play basketball, leaping and giggling in their black high-top sneakers.

Instead of the stone buildings, there are seven attached, two-story condominium units painted to look like small, eighteenth-century cottages, furnished with fake fireplaces and Sub-Zero refrigerators and Garland ovens.

When Mrs. Flax and my sister and I lived in Grove, high shrubs and a tall, latticework gate with a sign that read "Protectors of the Blessed Souls" separated our house from the convent. The shrubs have been cut back, and the gate and sign are gone now, replaced by a sign next to the driveway that reads, "No Children Under 12 Allowed."

I moved back to our old house on an April day when the forsythia blossoms were blowing yellow in the breeze. The house had been rented by a couple who were getting a divorce, and the woman was taking the kids and moving back to her parents' home in Montana.

The house feels more like a family to me than my family ever did. It is a gray, wood-frame house with a sagging front porch and old porch swing. I rented it furnished. The kitchen still has the red Formica table Joe was born beneath, the same table where Mrs. Flax served strange hors d'oeuvres for every meal. This house and property were owned by the convent and are now owned by the managing agent of the condominiums. I pay my rent, every month, to Colonial Gracious Homes.

I never cared much about furniture. The bureaus are the same ones that were in the house when we lived there years before, and the drawers smell of cloves; but the beds are new, from the store at the outlet center.

The kitchen is still painted yellow, like the forsythia, and still has the counters on which Mrs. Peretti made sauce from her tomatoes in the backyard and Mrs. Flax made more food from marshmallows than I care to recall.

Joe was also my school bus driver, and when I drove around with him after everybody else had been dropped off, he would tell me stories about that house—how his sisters used to stencil the windowpanes with sugar and water at Christmas time, and how they would line up their dolls on the steep stairway and make him jump over them.

Grove is a half hour south of "Woostah," spelled "Worcester," which is called the Heart of the Commonwealth. Grove has about 17,000 residents, and Main Street has a few stores left from the 1950s. If you squint as you drive down Main Street, you might think Grove is a quaint place, but then you see two X-rated video stores and a nail salon and coffee bar. The textile mills of the nineteenth century are, of course, gone, but, now, so is the cardboard box factory where so many people worked when we lived there. Now, there's an outlet center outside of town, where you can find people frantically looking for bargains at all hours of the night.

My son, Nick, was born not beneath a kitchen table, the way Joe Peretti was, but in a hospital in Eugene. He was born with a tiny hole in his heart. I raised Nick on my own in the misty rain of Eugene, and being a single mother felt almost normal to me, as I'd never been a mother any other way. Twice a week, I washed with cinnamon soap and spent time with the pediatric cardiologist in exchange for his services. The cardiologist would tell me about when he was a medical student in Croatia and slept on one of the tables in the library because he was so poor, and I would nod and imagine Joe telling me about how on the day his mother died he wandered around the house like a blind person.

In time, the hole in Nick's heart closed on its own, but that first year, every night, I would lean over Nick's crib by my bed and press my ear to his tiny chest to make sure he was still alive. Still, I could not make myself stop visiting the pediatric cardiologist, not for the whole time I lived in Eugene.

I never was one for going out at night much, even after my son grew up and moved away. What I like to do is look at slides I've taken, pictures of my past, projected on my bedroom wall. That and tai chi, which I learned as an undergraduate and practice in the morning, are the bookends of my days.

When Mrs. Flax and my sister and I lived in Grove, just being Jewish was enough to make us feel like immigrants. Now, I have students who speak eleven languages and don't know what the Mayflower was; each time I ask them, they think I'm giving them a botany quiz. Listening to them talk is like eavesdropping on an international party line. It crossed my mind to invite my students to the party I was planning for Mrs. Flax, but I did not. There are still people in Grove who do not look kindly on the Flax family, and not just because of what happened between me and Joe Peretti. I feel their looks and can almost see their gossip dripping down their collars when I go downtown. I didn't want to give them more to talk about.

So it will be a family party, and I will make a chocolate birthday cake with orange buttercream frosting. I like to bake, and I also specialize in fruit sandwiches—raspberry, blueberry, whatever is in season. You might think that after subsisting on Mrs. Flax's hors d'oeuvres I would have become more of a cook, but I cannot say I ever did.

My father, whom I always referred to as "Our Father Who Art in Heaven" when I was a child, disappeared before I was born. My sister Kate's father was a nice young man, as Mrs. Flax called him. I never met him, either. He was in St. Louis for swim races and was staying at the hotel where Mrs. Flax had a job as a chambermaid.

My son, Nick, seems to have his head screwed on fairly straight, although his childhood tendency to jump off the porch and scream, "I'm flying!" has grown into a passion for hang gliding off cliffs when he can afford it. He just graduated from college and immediately got work at Eastman Kodak in Rochester, New York. We never had twins in our family, so either his wife, Regina, took hormones the way everybody seems to do nowadays, or twins run in her family. Mrs. Flax, myself and now my son have all had babies when we were very young.

In recent years, Mrs. Flax has lived mostly in southern states, doing office work. She has written to me more than once of people she's met who refer to the Civil War as "the recent unpleasantness." She's currently in Atlanta, working at the *Atlanta Journal*. I keep track of her because she sends postcards, mostly pictures of interstates or gas stations from whatever state she's alighted in. She does not like to talk on the phone. On the last postcard she sent, of a Shell station in Georgia, she wrote, *Dear Charlotte, I love Atlanta. The newspa-*

per's slogan is "Covers Dixie like the Dew." She always signs her cards with x's and o's and then writes, *You Know Who.* Her old beau, Lou Landsky, still runs the shoe store in Grove, and Carrie says you can't buy a pair of shoes without him talking about Mrs. Flax's Lily of the Valley perfume.

Lou Landsky always said, "Ah clog zu Columbus"—"A curse on Columbus" in Yiddish—when he was startled by life. Lou Landsky knew about life. His wife left one day in the middle of vacuuming and didn't even turn off the machine. Other than Mrs. Flax, I don't know if he ever had another girlfriend, but I did see Mother Superior at the shoe store once. She came in with some young nun and sat in the graying black leather chair next to mine while Kate and I were trying on school shoes. Mr. Landsky went in the back and came out with two boxes of shoes balanced in one hand, like a waiter at an expensive restaurant. There were drops of water on the front of his white shirt, and his hair smelled of licorice and lemon drops as he sat on the stool in front of Mother Superior. He placed the boxes on the floor, then handed me two lollipops from his shirt pocket. I was so embarrassed, to get a lollipop right in front of the nuns.

After we left town in the middle of the night, I always imagined Lou Landsky standing on our front porch with a box in his hands, waiting for Mrs. Flax to return, endlessly waiting with a gift of a new pair of shiny high heels.

—🏠—

CHAPTER 3

"It is the fool's sheep that
break loose twice."

—Ghanaian Proverb

I drove home from school, parked in my driveway and
sat in my car with the motor turned off. I imagined I
could hear the nuns dribbling a basketball on the macadam court, the way I used to when they were out playing.
I thought of Joe Peretti's hands warming the back of my
neck, and I honked the horn three times the way he did
when I was late for the school bus. Then I looked down
at my book bag and thought about the aerogramme.

There were several things I could do with the aerogramme. I could just throw it in the outside trash cans.
It could be done in one swift move. Once, I threw away
a bag of fresh corn I'd just bought at the farmer's stand,
confusing it with the garbage. I could tear the letter up,

so there would be no possibility of ever knowing what it said. I could burn it in the fireplace without opening it. I could cross out my name and write "Return to Sender" on it and put it back in the mailbox—not my mailbox, but perhaps one in town; or I could drive farther, perhaps ten miles to a neighboring town, and put it in an anonymous mailbox there.

Did the post office send things all the way back across the ocean? And, if so, would the Sender have to pay the extra postage when the aerogramme showed up again in his post box in Leeds of all places?

I got out of the car, climbed the porch steps, sat down on the porch swing and slid the aerogramme out of my bag. Then I took out my old Swiss Army knife, which had belonged to my grandmother, not my grandfather, unfolded the small blade and carefully sliced open three sides of the envelope. Inside was a simple message:

Are you there?

Sorry for all these years.

Your father

I reached in my purse for another folded-up sheet of paper, a Xerox copy of a ripped-off part of a photograph showing a pair of men's brown lace-up shoes in yellow grass. Mrs. Flax had told me the shoes had belonged to my father. I'd carried the original torn piece of photograph around for years, until, one morning in Eugene, while I was giving Nick a bottle, I spilled a cup of coffee on it. Now, I carried the Xerox copy. It was the closest I had to something that had belonged to Mr. Flax. Sometimes I thought that if I hadn't been up in the bell tower that night with Joe and if Kate hadn't almost drowned, my father would have come back, that this was my punishment for my sin. Many times I thought he had died.

"It's hard to be rational with irrational people," I once read in a self-help book, a thought that really helped me in my dealings with Mrs. Flax. It did not help, though, when I was the one being irrational.

I was getting cold sitting on the porch swing holding the aerogramme and began to fumble for my keys, which I usually kept in an inner side pocket of my book bag. They weren't there. I marched back to the car, opened the door and searched the seats, but I could not find them. I rooted around in the glove compartment for a tissue, and, as I did, I heard the phone ringing in the house.

I ran around the back to the kitchen door. That door was locked, too, but I was able to yank open one of the back windows and climb in. The phone was still ringing when I landed on the kitchen floor, the same wall phone with a cord that had been there when I was a kid. But when I picked up the receiver, the line was dead.

One thing Mrs. Flax, Kate and I agreed on was we did not believe in microwaves. I used the microwave in the kitchen as a storage unit, and, although I wanted to toss the aerogramme back out the window, I did not. I put it to my lips to kiss it and smelled the paper again to see if I could summon any sense of this man who had left us. Then I carefully placed the letter in the microwave.

Mrs. Flax gave her full rendition of the disappearance of my father one winter morning when she was very much under the influence of vodka and ginger ale, sitting on the very porch in Grove where I opened the letter. She told the story as a series of numbered events, as if she were giving some kind of presentation at a meeting for abandoned wives, although I've never once seen her in that light and do not believe she has ever seen herself that way, either. I remember every word she said:

"One. We married and lived together for three months in a trailer. We hung leaves from the ceiling as decoration.

Two. I never loved anybody as much before or since.

Three. We used to fight a lot. He never physically hurt me, but once I threw a fork at him and it landed in his arm.

Four. He played the saxophone and dreamed of going to Hollywood, and he worked in the hardware store and he wrote poetry.

Five. I told him I was pregnant on the way to the supermarket. We went shopping. He paid for the food, and when we got to the car, he handed me the keys and said he was going to push the cart back to the store. I looked down to check my fingernails—I needed a manicure—and when I looked up he was gone. I waited an hour. That should have been a sign of things to come. But he met me at home. I don't know how he got there.

Six. When I was at the hospital, about to give birth to Charlotte Rose during the worst hailstorm in Chicago in five hundred years, he stole my car and I never saw him again. That's why I didn't put his name on the birth certificate. And that's why it is so important for you girls to learn to drive."

Many times after that, when I went to the supermarket, I would make one extra loop around the store in the hope that I would see my father's face, which would look exactly like mine, in the mirror above the vegetable bin, or even run into him at the checkout line.

With Joe, it was different. I never imagined seeing him again. With Joe, it was as if he'd never left; he was always with me.

The gossip was that when Joe fled Grove, he moved to Apalachicola, Florida, where his sisters lived, and they started selling Peretti's homemade tomato sauce. I admit, occasionally, I did check for a jar in the supermarket, but I never found it on the shelf.

The phone started ringing again, and this time I just reached over and picked it up after two rings. "Hello?" I said.

"Hello to you. Are you okay?" said a laughing voice.

It was Kate. She knew I had moved back to the house in Grove. She had driven off in the middle of the night eleven summers before in Oregon, after I'd yelled at her about the episode with the UPS man. I hadn't seen her since, but we had spoken many times.

"I'm very okay," I said, which is an expression one of my Greek students used.

"I have my kid with me," said Kate.

"What kid?" I demanded, catching my breath, leaning on the sink. I could hear a child shrieking in the background.

"My son," Kate said, and it sounded like she was joking, but this was her manner. "I have a son, too. He's three now." I could hear her trying to calm the boy down. "Irving, quiet, I'm on the phone."

"Irving?" Irving had been our grandfather's name. "You never told me you had a child. Where are you? You have a child named Irving?"

"It's a good way to honor the man. I've been in Houston, working in an E.R."

I never imagined Kate with a baby. Nick used to ask about it a lot when he was a child: "When is Aunt Kate going to have a baby?" or "Why doesn't Aunt Kate have a baby?"

I used to murmur things like, "She doesn't stay put long enough because she has the Mrs. Flax wandering gene," or "Maybe someday she will," although I never really believed that. When Kate was born, I wanted to name her after St. Gobnet, the virgin beekeeper saint, which would not have been appropriate. God knows, Kate was sexually active. That was the term now. When we were younger, people called her "fast." If you said that about a girl now, people would think she ran track.

Back then, it meant Kate didn't wear underwear. She was one of those girls who just thought, what's the point? But here Kate was on the phone, with a child named Irving.

"How old did you say he is?" I asked.

"I told you, he's three. He's a good kid. He eats sticks, but otherwise he's a good kid."

"What do you mean he eats sticks?" I said, pulling the phone away from my ear and staring at it.

"Well, he chews on them," said Kate.

When Nick's father, Bill, was still in the picture, enough for me to do his laundry, before Nick was conceived, Kate came to visit us in Eugene. I was folding clothes on top of the dryer when she arrived.

"Oh, Charlotte," said Kate as she lifted up a pair of Bill's boxers and held them to her face. "What joy."

I snatched them away. "Keep your joy to yourself," I said, and grabbed the stack of underwear.

"Oh, Charlotte," she said. "You have to live a little."

"Well, who's the father?" I asked, putting the phone back to my ear.

"Who said anything about a father?" said Kate.

"Are you kidding me? Who takes care of him while you're at work?"

"Day care," said Kate, sounding annoyed. She did not want to discuss the father question. "Is it okay if I bring Irving to the party?"

"He's my nephew!" I shouted. "I want to meet my nephew!"

"Great," said Kate. "We'll be there. We can stay with you, right? There's room. There have been kids in that house before. The Peretti girls and Joe when he was a baby?"

"Right," I said, a little queasy.

Irving was shrieking in the background again. "I have to go," said Kate, and she hung up.

I stood there, dazed, and stared at the "Living Simply" calendar with photos of New England life that the last tenants had put up on the wall. There were quotes for each month about living a simple life. July's quote was "A contented heart is an even sea in the midst of all storms."

I could not believe Kate had a son, a boy who ate sticks.

I opened the refrigerator and took out a pint of sour cream. I carried it to the kitchen sink, peeled off the lid, stuck my hand in the white stuff and patted it neatly all over my face. Carrie swore that a sour-cream mask made skin smoother than any of that high-end stuff.

Carrie and her husband, Tim, and their son, Kenneth, lived in what we used to call a modern house. There was a lot of glass, and it was always freezing cold in January and steaming hot in the summertime. Kenneth had gone to the special school for children who'd been thrown out of public school. We all called it the Throwaway School. On the cover of the school handbook was a quote that read in italics, *"All of us broken, none of us insignificant."* I now wondered if they had ever had a boy who ate sticks.

We had to do ten hours of community service to pass the ninth grade at Grove High. The Throwaway School always seemed to be in session, so on the days off from public school, I'd be there trying patiently to tie the bow on the dress of Jerome, who liked to cross-dress at age eight, or holding the hand of Anthony, the boy with one arm.

One day Jerome shrieked with horror as he sat down at the manual typewriter, "Charlotte Flax! This typewriter ain't got no z!"

"Don't mind him," said Anthony, swirling the index finger of his one hand toward his head. "He's a little here and there. But you! You're a cupcake!"

At that point Jerome jumped up and shook a long fingernail at Anthony. "She ain't no cupcake!" he said, waving his hand at me. "She's a lovely cupcake," which I do believe is the best compliment anybody has ever given me in my life so far.

One day Carrie came to pick up Kenneth while I was there. He was standing in the corner wearing his thick black glasses and saluted when he saw his mother. He never blinked, you could see that even through those glasses, but Carrie went over to him and cradled that boy in her arms like he was Baby Jesus himself. Now, remarkably, Kenneth was serving in the Army in Kuwait.

I stood staring out the kitchen window into the dusk for ten minutes, then scrubbed the mask off and sat like a statue on the living room couch, watching the Weather Channel, the reports of record high and low temperatures around the world. I had the unsettling but certain feeling, the way you know it's going to rain when the leaves blow in the wind and show their undersides, that Kate would be arriving soon, with little Irving, who ate sticks.

—⌂—

CHAPTER 4

"The green new broom
sweepeth clean the home."

—English Proverb

The morning after Kate called with her Irving news, I stood at the kitchen sink eating a juicy strawberry sandwich, letting the juice drip down my chin.

My mind drifted to Joe Peretti unbuttoning my blouse, his hands chapped from pulling on the hemp bell rope. I was slurping the strawberries and staring down at the mess in the sink when there was a knock at the kitchen door.

I wiped my face with my hand and felt my teeth for strawberry seeds, then went to see who was there.

Through the screen, I could see Kate holding a robust, jolly little boy with red curls wearing blue-jean overalls, a small green t-shirt and construction boots—

and, indeed, he was holding a stick with some bark left on it. Here was my nephew, Irving. Here was my sister, Kate, after all these years. I wanted to hug both of them, but I kept my arms tight at my sides.

"Come in, come in! Let me meet this guy!" I sputtered. What else could I say, an adorable chubby boy reaching out to me—and I reached out to him like we'd been waiting for each other forever. But Kate and I could not look each other in the eye.

"See?" said Kate. She was disheveled but sexy the way she always was in her tight white v-neck t-shirt and very short blue-jean shorts, showing no signs of childbirth. Maybe her thighs were a bit thicker and her hair was a darker shade of red, but she moved with the same physical confidence she'd always had. It didn't seem possible we hadn't seen each other in more than a decade.

"See what?" I said, as Irving swung his stick around, practically poking me in the eye.

I flinched, and Kate and I smiled at each other.

"Skibbee," said Irving.

"He means, 'Excuse me,'" said Kate.

I carried Irving into the living room, and he immediately squirmed down and headed for the stairs as I peeked out the front window. Kate's 1987 green Honda Civic was in the driveway.

"I have some jars of barbecue sauce, if you know anybody who could use them," she said. "Lots of cilantro and peppers," as if we were picking up a conversation from yesterday.

"How could you not have told me about him!" I said.

"He never stops," said Kate, as she headed up the stairs after her son. "I barely have enough time to take a shower."

"Well, who's the father?" I demanded, clambering up the stairs after her.

Kate shrugged. Irving was in the bathroom, about to put a box of Kleenex in the toilet.

"I didn't get him at the 7-Eleven," said Kate, pulling him away. "Look at him. He's got our eyebrows."

It was true. In addition to having Kate's red, curly hair, he had the same thick eyebrows that all us Flax women have.

We herded Irving downstairs, and Kate and I sat at the kitchen table as Irving tried to open the refrigerator, still clutching his stick in his right fist.

"Does he ever put the stick down?" I asked.

"When he finds another one," said Kate.

"You said he ate them."

On cue, as if Irving knew what he was supposed to do, he started chewing on the side of the stick.

"That's not good," I said.

"There are worse things," said Kate. "Some kids eat dirt."

"I got a letter from Our Father Who Art in Heaven," I said, my eyes on Irving.

"Well, invite him to the birthday party," said Kate, getting up to open the refrigerator and see what was inside.

I glared at her back. "I will *not* invite that man to the party," I said, surprised at my own ferocity.

"But that's what you *should* do," said Kate, turning to face me and matching my tone. We were suddenly so angry that Irving stopped gnawing on his stick and looked up at us like he was going to cry, so we shut up.

"Does Irving still sleep in a crib?" I asked.

"He never did," said Kate. "He likes a mattress on the floor. I have a small one in the car."

"Fine," I said. "You can set that up in the guest room—Mrs. Flax's old room. The bed is made up there. I'll be back in an hour or so. I have a meeting at the college."

Kate raised her eyebrows, but I ignored her. The fact was I needed to go swimming. When Kate had given up the sport, I had taken it up. Now, I often feel a need to get my fins wet. When I dive into the water, I could swear I sprout gills. I feel more comfortable in the water in my aqua Speedo than I do on land in my clothes. Swimming laps, I feel like I used to when I swung on the rope swing that hung from a branch of a tree behind our house when we lived in either Montana or Nebraska. I flew in that swing, in summer over the lime-lit grass, and in wintertime when it was sugared in snow.

I drove off to the YMCA, trying to steady my nerves, praying that Kate would not cause trouble the way she always did.

At the pool, I recognized one other woman swimming—exotic Lenore, doing the breaststroke in her chic matching navy blue bathing suit and bathing cap. Seeing me as her head bobbed up, she smiled and waved. Lenore works at one of the two banks in Grove. She and her husband moved to town just after they had their third child. A few months later, her husband was killed in a car crash out by the outlet center.

Lenore is one of the few other Jews in town. She and I had said hello a few weeks before in the locker room and were beginning to be friends.

We swam next to each other for a while, like seahorses in a race with no finish line.

After my swim, I put my bathing suit in the special spin dryer, which is like a salad spinner for bathing suits. As the excess water was spun out, I tried to believe all was right with the world.

In the locker room, women called to one another over the lockers, as if they were hanging clothes on clotheslines in the countryside, muttering about heartbreak and politics and sharing telephone numbers of acupuncturists. I said hello to Dee, standing naked at a mirror, drying her hair. Dee is almost six feet tall and skinny as a straw. She was in the class ahead of me when I was in ninth grade at Grove High. The first day of school after President Kennedy was shot, she offered me her Ring-Dings at lunch, so I considered her a generous person. Now, the only facilities Dee uses at the Y are the showers. She spends her days poling around town on cross-country skis with wheels and washes her husband's clothes in their bathtub.

I drove home from the pool smelling of chlorine, the

way Kate always did as a child. I admit I liked seeing lights on when I got back and being able to pretend there was something normal about my family.

Kate and Irving hadn't eaten, so I made a box of macaroni and cheese that had been in the cupboard when I moved in. Irving sat on a regular chair without falling off, his fork in one hand and his stick in the other. He ate the macaroni and cheese and only put the stick in his mouth once.

"Skibbee," he said every once in a while, and, "I want cars."

"That was his first sentence," said Kate. "'I want cars.'"

I nodded. I wanted to show her the letter and opened my mouth to raise the subject of Our Father Who Art in Heaven again, but I couldn't bring myself to do it.

"Why did you want to be a nun?" Kate asked, helping herself to the last of the macaroni.

I wasn't expecting that. All the years we had lived with Mrs. Flax, Kate had never asked me that question—not that I could have explained if she had asked. I still couldn't.

The year before Kate was born, when we lived in Ellenboro, Wisconsin, I saw a girl with ashes on her forehead cross herself and chant Hail Marys before a spelling bee, and I was hooked. The next day, I stole an old piece of charcoal from a neighbor's grill and walked around with a smudge between my eyebrows for a week and a half. For years after that, I tried to read the New

Testament to Kate as her bedtime story, but she didn't buy it, and it drove Mrs. Flax crazy. Kate, even with her mouth full, did a good imitation of Mrs. Flax saying, "For God's sakes, Charlotte! You're Jewish! For God's sakes!"

I didn't answer. I just took my time scraping up the last bit of macaroni and cheese on my plate with my fork.

"Kate," I blurted. "Who's the father?"

"What difference does it make?" Kate said angrily, jumping up with her plate as if she was going to run out of the house.

I grabbed the short sleeve of her tight, white t-shirt, and she stopped and put her plate back down on the table.

"Who is it?" I asked again.

Kate shrugged and sat down. "E.M.S. guy I met in Houston. I liked my place there. I had wind chimes."

I nodded. "I like wind chimes. Is the father married to somebody else?"

She stared at her plate and twirled her fork. "I thought he was going to leave her," she said softly.

"Has he seen *him*?" I nodded toward Irving.

"I want cars," said Irving.

Kate shook her head, and I sighed and said, "Join the club."

"Actually, do you have any toy cars?" she asked.

"No," I said, "but we could go sit in a real car. I used to do that with Nick."

Then Kate started singing "Frère Jacques" to Irving and I joined in, and we didn't speak anymore about the E.M.S guy.

We went out to my car, I opened the door on the driver's side, and Irving scrambled in and grabbed the wheel, still clutching his stick in one hand. I went around to the passenger side, and Kate got in back.

"I want cars! I want cars!" Irving screamed, bouncing up and down. I reached over and took the car keys out of the ignition, and Kate and I sat silently while Irving bounced and yelled.

This went on for almost half an hour, until suddenly he put his head down on the steering wheel and closed his eyes.

Kate got out of the back seat, came around to the driver's side, opened the door, lifted Irving up and carefully carried him into the house. I followed her upstairs and watched as she lay him down on the little mattress in their room and covered him with a small blanket. Then I went to my room, the room that had once been Joe Peretti's room, the room where Kate and I had once slept in bunk beds, the room where I had slept alone in Kate's upper bunk the night I lost my virginity and Kate almost drowned.

CHAPTER 5

"A dimple in the chin,
a devil within."

—Irish Proverb

The next morning was a blazing hot summer day, and at breakfast Irving managed to pull a container of orange juice out of the refrigerator as Kate and I sipped our coffee. I was able to grab it just as he began to pour the juice on the floor.

Kate tore off some paper towels and knelt down to mop up the mess. I opened the door of the microwave and took out the aerogramme.

"Here it is," I said, waving the pale blue paper in her face.

Kate reached up with one hand and snatched it and studied the words.

"Why the hell not? Invite the man," she said, handing

the letter back to me. "Always good to have extra men," she added, sounding exactly like Mrs. Flax.

I put the aerogramme back in the microwave, and then I did what I swore I would never do. I grabbed a pen from the coffee can I kept near the stove, took a piece of lined paper from the pad on the counter and sat down at the kitchen table to write back to my father.

Dear Mr, I began, but his name wasn't Flax. I didn't know what it was. I crumpled up that sheet of paper and ripped another from the pad.

Hello, I wrote, and on the next line: *Good to hear from you. We're having a party for,* and then I wrote, *my mother,* which was a word I rarely spoke or wrote. *You're welcome.* I crossed that out and wrote, *You are welcome,* without the contraction, but that seemed extreme, so I ripped that up and wrote another note saying, *You're welcome. It's on Labor Day, September 2nd.* And then I wrote:

RSVP

Sincerely,

Charlotte

I considered telling him I had a son, which meant he had a grandson. I even considered telling him my son had children, which made him a great-grandfather, but I thought if he surfaced there would be time for that.

I checked my watch. "I have some errands to do," I said suddenly to Kate, who was now dealing with Irving as he ran around the kitchen with his stick.

In fact, it was Wednesday and nearing "ten o'clock

a.m." as my student Darius had put it when he invited me for coffee at his house. I can honestly say I had never socialized with any of my students and had never gone to a student's house for coffee or any other drink. I had always found a polite way to decline these invitations, but not this time. "I am waiting for you," Darius had said.

Taking a shower, I felt like I was in some kind of a trance, the way I used to feel when I got ready to meet Nick's cardiologist.

After I dried off, I put on fairly clean jeans, a bra that wasn't too stretched out, a sleeveless blouse, flat sandals and lipstick. Kate watched me apply the lipstick with one eyebrow raised. She was on the porch with Irving when I drove off, and I could see her in the rearview mirror, shaking her head.

Darius lived two towns away. I drove out into the summer morning to 113 Laurel Lane, the address on his card. I had no trouble finding it. I'd been in the area many times years before. It was part of the school bus route I rode with Joe Peretti when we dropped off all the other kids.

The house was a two-story stucco, nothing dramatic, with a neatly trimmed front lawn. There was a baseball bat under the hedge along the driveway and a dark red SUV in the open garage. I parked on the street, pinched my cheeks the way Mrs. Flax always did when she went on a date when Kate and I were kids, tilted down the rearview mirror and put on fresh lipstick, then walked up the path to the front door.

I rang the doorbell—it sounded like a cuckoo clock—
and a few moments later, there was handsome Darius at
the door. He was wearing jeans and a navy blue t-shirt with
the word "Firsts" across the front, and he was barefoot.

"Thank you for coming," he said with that trace of
an Eastern European accent, shaking my hand. Now, it
felt like he was the teacher.

He swept his arm grandly, gesturing me inside, like
he was going to give me a tour of a castle, but, in fact,
the house looked like it had been robbed by very neat
thieves. There was no couch in the living room, only two
leather armchairs and a turquoise lawn chair arranged
around a coffee table with shell fossils displayed in a
circle on top. A few framed watercolors and family pho-
tographs hung on the walls, which were marked with
empty rectangles where other pictures once had hung.

"Please, sit," Darius said, and I hesitantly sat down
on the lawn chair, perching primly on the edge of the
seat. He sat down on a leather chair next to me. Now,
I wasn't quite sure why I was there, and my heart was
racing, and I wondered if I was going to have sex with
my student.

"I study firsts," he said, smiling and pointing to his
t-shirt.

I nodded, although I wasn't sure what he was getting
at.

"Twelve hundred years ago, monks first recorded
the flowering of the cherry blossoms in Kyoto," he said.
"I also do construction. Would you like some coffee?"

It occurred to me then that this man might actually just want to talk.

And then he blurted, "I am still in love with my wife. My ex-wife." He pointed to a framed photograph of himself and a bosomy blond woman standing on either side of a slender, fair-haired boy. "She took half the furniture," he said, gesturing around in the room. "I met her, Liselle, in Poland. She became a real estate agent here after our son started high school, and she began to see the bigger houses with the Jacuzzis in their bathrooms and the family rooms over their garages. 'Frogs,' she said they are called. Do you know this word?"

"No," I said. "I don't know about that kind of frogs."

"Liselle had clients who lived in one of these big houses. McMansions, she called them. Do you know this word?"

"Yes." I nodded. That one I knew.

"The owners said they wanted to sell the house. Liselle was helping them. After a while, she began to say things like, "As soon as we sell the house"—as if it was *her* house. By the time the owners were ready to sell it, Liselle had been many times in the big bedroom with the husband."

Darius stopped speaking and dropped his head. There was something about him that reminded me of Joe, an honesty and vulnerability I found endearing.

"The man divorced his wife," Darius continued. "Liselle divorced me, and now she is the second wife of a man with a 'frog.'"

"I'm sorry," I said.

"Thank you for coming," said Darius, standing up suddenly.

I was startled. We hadn't even had coffee, but Darius headed up the stairs and made no sign for me to follow.

I called up after him, "Thank you! Thank you for the visit!" And then I let myself out.

I had seen a lot, but this was something a bit different. I was very attracted to this man, but I had told myself I was not going to get into another relationship, and certainly not with a student. Now, it seemed this would not be an issue. The man just wanted to talk. Perhaps he really wanted to practice his English.

I hurried out to my car and sped off. I usually drive slowly, so slowly that Mrs. Flax would say, "Charlotte, you drive like something's wrong with your mind." But, this time, I wanted to get away.

I am not good at driving fast. Racing back to Grove, I suddenly saw a flashing red light in my rearview mirror. A police car was following me. My stomach sank and my heart started beating faster, and then I heard a police officer say through the loudspeaker, "Pull over!"

I pulled over, and the police car drove up behind me, light still flashing.

The policeman got out of his car and walked toward me. I rolled down my window.

When I looked up at him, I realized I knew this guy, even with his uniform and sunglasses and belly and badge. It was Kevin O'Neil. I'd gone to school with him in ninth grade. Kevin had not been nice to me when I returned to school after Kate had almost drowned and everyone knew it was because I'd been up in the bell tower with Joe Peretti and Joe had left town.

Kevin recognized me, too.

"Well, Charlotte Flax," he said. "May I see your registration? You Flaxes back for more trouble?"

"Hi, Kevin, we're not," I said, reaching for the glove compartment. I actually found the registration, and it was good through 1991.

I handed Kevin the card. He examined it, frowning.

"Well, slow down," Kevin said, handing it back.

I did not say to him, "There was no need to hang size-large ladies' black lace underpants on my locker."

Instead I said, "Thank you, Officer" and drove slow as a snail the rest of the way home.

CHAPTER 6

"Love rules
without rules."

—Italian Proverb

The following day, Darius sat in the front row in my
English language class, and I could barely concentrate, so I gave the students an exercise I'd learned in
Eugene. I told them to pair up, face their partner, hold
hands, make as much eye contact as possible and take
turns saying, "I thank you for your trust."

It was one of the stupidest exercises I'd ever given
them, but I wanted them to be too busy focusing on each
other to pay any attention to me, and it worked. Darius
paired up with my Greek student who liked to say, "I'm
very okay," and they started talking about soccer. Watching Darius, I found myself thinking for the first time that
maybe I could fall in love with someone besides Joe, but I

knew that a student was not an intelligent choice.

As the students filed out at the end of the class, Darius slipped me a note that read, *Thank you for listening to my woes. I will have a better date for you tonight at 8 p.m. Please visit me.*

When I returned home, I found the *Grove Sentinel,* furled and lying like a fish on the front step. I didn't want to go inside yet, so I picked it up and sat on the porch swing reading the newspaper. There was a short piece on a total solar eclipse that had been visible earlier that day from Hawaii down through Mexico.

When I was a small child, two hands had put special cardboard glasses with dark film lenses over my eyes so I wouldn't be blinded by an eclipse of the sun when I stared up at the sky. I always believed they were my father's hands, though I was aware I could be wrong.

I got up and went inside and found Kate trying to feed Irving, who was marching around the kitchen with his stick, shouting, "More! More! More cars!"

I dropped the newspaper on the table, but Kate and I didn't speak. I went to my room and twisted on my bed for a while, trying to sleep, then got up and went back to the kitchen.

"I'm going to make a loaf of dill bread," I said to Kate, who was reading the paper or pretending to, but she just nodded. Irving kept lunging with his stick at the bowl of batter, but I managed to put the pan into the oven without any accidents.

Then, with my back to Kate, I said, "There's a big

sale on kids clothes at Kmart. I'll be back soon. I've set the timer. You be sure and take the bread out, okay?"

Kate stayed sitting at the kitchen table, flipping through the paper as Irving ran around with his stick in one hand and a sippy cup of milk in the other. She nodded but did not look up at me. Instead, she quietly recited a line I'd once told her Nick had come home with in second grade: "Life is like a penis. Sometimes it's hard."

I drove slowly through Grove back to Darius's house. When I got there, I parked in the driveway, turned off the motor, then smoothed my eyebrows in the rearview mirror and pinched my cheeks. As I looked at myself in the mirror, I remembered the first time I felt sexual stirrings, when I was in fifth grade in Montana and an eye doctor touched my head.

I had been sent for an eye exam because of an incident in geography class. We were studying the voyage of Christopher Columbus, and our teacher, Miss Rae, had carefully drawn three little boats on the blackboard in pink chalk, each sailing wildly into the unknown with its name written on the bow. I knew, of course, that they were the Nina, the Pinta and the Santa Maria, but when Miss Rae asked me what they were, I thought it was a trick question. The pink chalk made the boats look like flowers, so I answered, "Flowers?"

All the kids laughed, and Miss Rae said in front of the whole class that either I was stupid or I had vision troubles, and she thought it was the latter. When she said "latter" I heard "ladder" and pictured someone putting a miniature ladder in my brain.

Mrs. Flax took me to the local eye doctor, Dr. Diamond. He was a quiet man in a darkened office, and when he told me to put my eyes up to that machine with lenses and touched the top of my head, I felt stirrings.

"Is this better or is this better? Is this better or is this better?" he asked as he switched the lenses and I squirmed and strained to read the faraway letters. I thought of Dr. Diamond as I walked up the walk to Darius's front door and knocked.

"Come in," I heard Darius say.

I turned the handle, and the door was indeed unlocked. I opened it and stepped inside, and there he was, grinning. He pulled me behind the door, like we were in a crazy cartoon, and we stayed there with the door open, hidden behind it. He put his hands on my shoulders and gently pushed me down, and I stayed there like that, taking him in, as cars rushed by outside.

And then I stood up and he lifted my skirt, pushed my underwear aside and pulled me to him, lifting my leg. He was in me as the phone rang and cars drove by outside. There was no mention of a condom. I did not use good judgment, as they say.

Darius managed to push the door shut and we collapsed right there in the front hall, on the red-and-white hooked rug.

Afterward, we got up and put ourselves together, and he led me to the upstairs bathroom. I did not love this man. He did not love me. That was not what this was about. This was like what I had done with the cardiologist.

We undressed, he gave me a shower cap, and we stepped into the shower together.

As we were drying off, he said, "I've made coffee."

"No, thank you. I shouldn't do this," I said as I got dressed. "I need my job."

Darius did not say a word.

As I drove home, I tried to smooth my hair in the rearview mirror. I drove a tiny bit above the speed limit, and, thankfully, Officer Kevin O'Neil was nowhere in sight.

Coming up the driveway, I saw that all the lights in the house were on, like Kate was having a party. I parked, flicked on the overhead car light and examined my face in the rearview mirror. I looked alive, I had to say that.

I went inside and found Kate still at the kitchen table with the newspaper in front of her, with Irving asleep on the floor at her feet. The smell of fresh dill bread filled the house.

"Never too late for kids clothes," Kate said drily, surveying my tousled hair.

"They were all out," I mumbled. "Thanks for taking out the bread," I said, pressing my fingers to the top of the warm loaf on the counter. I tiptoed to the hall closet, where I kept my camera, and took it out quietly. Then I tiptoed back into the kitchen and took several photos of Irving, who looked like a fallen angel.

"How about me?" said Kate, unbuttoning her blouse and flashing her breasts.

I put down my camera.

"What the hell are you doing?" I hissed, trying not to wake Irving.

"I still have beautiful breasts, don't you think?" she said, sticking out her chest.

She did, but I wasn't going to tell her that. I clenched my teeth and stomped upstairs.

That night, when I woke up, I didn't look at slides. I didn't want to while Kate was in the house. She would just laugh at me the way she had once laughed at a picnic when I ate a whole hamburger and part of the soggy paper plate underneath it before I realized I was chewing cardboard.

I needed something else to do, so I picked up the spiral notebook I kept by the bed, opened it to a clean page and started making a list:

PARTY

1. Order food
2. Decide on music
3. Toy trucks for Irving
4. New dress
5. Underwear

The next day at school I met privately with a young woman from Brazil who couldn't stop crying because she hadn't been able to go back for her sister's funeral. Her sister had died during some kind of plastic surgery gone wrong.

Then I had my English language class. Darius was already sitting in the front row when I walked in. I handed out copies of the lyrics to "This Land is Your Land." I often had my students sing folk songs to help them learn more English and feel like part of the community. They always enjoyed it, and I enjoyed watching Darius read the lyrics as we sang a fairly rousing rendition of the song. But then Darius made me blush by looking up and actually winking at me.

I wanted to flee the room, but I had already done that once and didn't want to make a habit of it. Finally, the class ended, and the students began gathering their things and leaving. I was at my desk, stacking the essays I'd asked them to write about their favorite childhood desserts when Kate appeared, breathless, dragging Irving by the hand.

"The car seat is in the hall," she said, pulling Irving forward to hand him to me.

Darius came up behind me and pressed his body against my back. "This is your grandson?" he asked, stepping around me and bowing formally as he took Irving's tiny hand.

"Skibbee," said Irving.

"This is my nephew," I said.

"I have a dentist's appointment," said Kate, lifting Irving off the floor and standing him on top of the stack of papers on my desk. I grabbed him just as he was starting to topple over.

The remaining students looked as stunned as I was. I didn't know if it was because they had seen Darius press up against me, or because Irving was in my arms, waving his stick like a little orchestra conductor, or because of the impression Kate made entering and now leaving. Whatever the reason, they clustered around for a while and even took turns holding Irving until he squirmed down.

When I finally said I needed to be going, Darius followed me out of the room and down the hall, walking closely behind me carrying the car seat. I felt like we were a small family, about to go somewhere together, but then he deftly installed the car seat in the back seat of my car, bowed and said solemnly, "Have a good voyage."

He leaned over as I strapped Irving into the car seat and whispered in my ear, "I will see you tonight at eleven p.m. at the all-night mattress store."

I struggled with Irving and the little straps for a while longer, trying not to get my eye poked out with his stick. Then I got in the front seat, adjusted the rearview mirror and turned to look at Darius. For a moment, I imagined being married to a man like him and what it would have been like to have had someone to help me with Nick all those years.

It was true, there was an all-night mattress store in the outlet mall, neither of which had been there in the early '60s. I had never been in it, but I knew exactly where it was.

Halfway home, I suddenly missed my son so much that I pulled into a gas station and called him from an outdoor phone booth, so I could keep an eye on Irving.

"Hello?" I said as soon I heard someone pick up the phone. "Hello, Nick?"

The twins were shouting in the background.

"Hi, Mom! Where are you?"

"I'm at work," I lied. "Your grandfather might be coming to the party," I said, but my son could not hear me over the household din.

"What?" he said.

"I said your grandfather, my father, might be coming to the party!"

There was a brief silence, and then Nick yelled, "That's great! I've always wanted to meet the guy!"

"I have, too," I said quietly. And then, more loudly, "And Kate has a son! They're here! His name is Irving, and he's three years old!"

"That should be interesting," said Nick. "A cousin. Wow. Hey, I got some great pictures of my last flight."

"You know I don't like you jumping off cliffs like that," I sighed. In the car, Irving was contentedly chewing on his stick.

"You should try it, Mom," he said. "Come on up and I'll take you sometime."

These were lines we had spoken many times before, and I said what I always said next: "No thank you, dear. I don't think humans are meant to fly."

I asked about the twins and Regina, and he said they were fine, and then we hung up, and I stood by the phone booth in the heat for a while, wishing Mother Superior were there to help me deal with missing Nick so much. I felt the way I did when I went to her hoping for guidance about Joe Peretti and she told me about her brother who had worked in a wholesale place that sold spices from wooden barrels and would come home with paprika on his shoes and cinnamon sticks in his pockets that she would put under her pillow. When he left that job, he had joined the Army and had been killed some time between World War I and World War II. Nobody knew how. He was only seventeen years old, and they sent him home in pieces in a box.

I knew Mother Superior would not actually be of help now, but I longed for her anyway. It was then that I picked up the phone again and called Cooks Inn.

"I'd like to reserve a room for Labor Day weekend," I said to the woman who answered. "Two nights, Sunday and Monday. For Flax. Leonard Flax."

I felt a shiver as I said this name. I did not know if my father would actually come to the party, or how long he would stay if he did come, and I did not know his name, first or last, but it was the first time in my life that I had even pretended to know and say his name out loud.

There were still seven weeks until Mrs. Flax's party, but I couldn't stop thinking about it. Perhaps other people would not think a sixtieth birthday party for their mother would change their lives, but I did. All my life, I had felt like our family of Mrs. Flax and Kate and me had been on a ship without a captain drifting toward a dangerous waterfall. I had a fantasy that at this party I might finally be able to turn the ship around.

CHAPTER 7

"Act quickly, think slowly."

—Greek Proverb

On the way to school that day, I had stopped at Kmart and bought a toy cement mixer and a toy fire truck with doors that opened, which I knew was a crucial feature for young boys. When I got home after class with Irving, I took the bag out of the car trunk, lifted Irving out of his car seat and started up the porch steps. There was another postcard in the mailbox from Mrs. Flax with a picture of a water tower in the shape of a peach. She had scrawled across the back, *Don't you just love it? Can't wait 'til my Sweet 16! XOXO, You Know Who.*

There was also a large manila envelope wedged between the screen door and the front door. I snatched it and looked at the return address as I dug for my keys: Colonial Gracious Homes.

I didn't need my keys. The door was unlocked. I thought I'd have to talk to Kate about that when she got back from the dentist, but when I went inside, Kate was there, looking like she was dressed for a date in a very tight, short, low-cut orange dress that barely covered anything.

"I have things to do," said Kate. "Could you watch him for a while?" She headed for the door as Irving headed for a container of Play-Doh on the coffee table.

"I have things to do, too," I said, bending down to pick bits of turquoise Play-Doh off the rug. "Where are you going?"

"There's an E.R. in Crompton. I have friends there, and they say I can work a shift." Kate stopped and looked me in the eye, something she rarely did. "I need to," she said. "I need to work in E.R.'s. I need the action. You wouldn't understand."

And then she turned and ran out the door.

Irving shouted, "Get cars!" and dumped the whole container of Play-Doh on the rug. I took the fire truck and cement mixer out of the bag and set them down.

"Drive!" Irving shouted, dropping his stick for a moment. He took a vehicle in each hand and began crashing them together as I ripped open the envelope and read the letter inside:

Dear Guest,
We have great news! Colonial Gracious Homes will soon be a gated community. Expansion-and-improvement plans include building three new con-

dominium units and converting the residence at 4 Harvest Road into a front office and guardhouse, to be operational by January 1, 1992.

This work requires that you vacate the premises by December 1, 1991. If you would like to remain a part of the Colonial Gracious Homes community, we invite you to consider purchasing one of our new luxury condominiums and will be happy to meet with you to discuss financing.

Please contact our office at your earliest convenience.

I read the letter and then read it again. I couldn't believe it. I was being kicked out! I picked up the phone to call Carrie but hung up, thinking that if I didn't talk about the letter, there was still a chance it didn't really exist.

Joe once told me about a river somewhere that somebody decided to reroute right through a town so that most of the neighborhoods would end up underwater. The townspeople seemed to go insane, he said. They stopped mowing their lawns. They began sleeping with their next-door neighbors. That's how I felt after reading the Colonial Gracious Homes letter, like I had become unhinged.

Gut this house? This was the house where Joe had helped his mother make tomato sauce, splitting the tomatoes and popping them out of their skins so the seeds filled his fingernails. Joe had told me during one of our bus rides that his parents had been married in November and so had all their friends. They all used to sit around the kitchen table on Saturday nights, playing cards— the same kitchen table I still sat at—the women in their print dresses, the men in their undershirts. "Joey," his father would say, hitting him on the head, "Joey, maybe some day you'll grow up and join the November Club."

Turn the convent grounds into a gated community? This was where I had planted a pumpkin patch when I was fourteen. I'd buried the seeds, smooth and white, in the woods behind the house, but I never knew if any of them had sprouted. We had moved soon after, and I couldn't remember where I'd planted them now.

My eyes started to water. I picked up Irving, who now had the cement mixer in one hand and his stick in the other, and hurried out the kitchen door and across the backyard into the hot summer woods, stumbling and crying, search- ing for a stray pumpkin. I did not have a clue where to look. I hugged Irving close, but he wriggled down and insisted on walking. I gripped his hand tight as we circled the pond.

At ten-thirty that night, I was in my room, standing na- ked in front of the mirror, holding a breast in each hand when Kate barged in with Irving and his stick.

"What the hell are you doing?" she hissed, putting a hand over Irving's eyes. "What kind of role model are you?"

"Get out!" I yelled. "Don't you know how to knock?"

"So you have a date," she said, slamming the door as she left.

"No! I don't have a date!" I yelled. "I'm going swimming! I'm just thinking if I need a new bathing suit!"

Kate didn't respond, but I heard her walking down the stairs.

Ten minutes later, I was wearing almost-matching beige underwear and a beige bra, a yellow summer dress I'd bought a few years before and beige sandals. The dress was a little tight, but it still worked.

I drove out toward the mall, feeling like a magnet was pulling me. The parking lot wasn't totally empty. There were about six cars. Employees, maybe. Or people who worked long hours and could only shop late. Or people who just wanted to cool off in the air-conditioning.

I stood outside the all-night mattress place, trying to act casual, like I had a reason to be there. I did my tai chi breathing and then walked into the extremely air-conditioned store. There were about thirty beds on the showroom floor—singles and doubles and queens and kings—and there was Darius, in jeans and a white t-shirt, lying on his back on a big circular bed with his arms behind his head and a picture of a large crown hanging on the wall behind him. His running shoes were placed neatly on the floor beside the bed, like he lived there.

He didn't sit up when he saw me, just patted the bed and said, "Come, Miss Charlotte. You lie here. Take off your shoes and lie here."

I cannot say I hesitated. I slipped off my sandals and put them neatly beside his shoes and lay down next to him. Not so our bodies were touching, but next to him.

He immediately moved over and slid his hand under my back and somehow, through my dress, unhooked my bra.

"Darius, stop," I said, at which point a young woman wearing a blue smock and a big button that read "Sleep with Us 24 Hours a Day" came rushing over.

"Is everything okay over here?" she asked, her long blond hair falling in front of her face. She looked familiar, and then I recognized her. It was Nancy Hines, who worked in the cafeteria at school.

"Oh, we're fine, Nancy," I said, sitting up quickly with my arms tightly crossed over my chest.

"You!" she said, looking first at Darius and then at me. I wasn't sure which one of us she meant or which of us she was more surprised to see with the other.

"This is our most expensive bed," Nancy said, nodding toward the mattress and going into her sales pitch, even though she still looked completely shocked. "My mother likes it, too," she babbled. "She always says when she comes to pick me up, 'If that circle bed ever goes on sale, let me know.' I tell her, 'It's "circular," Mom, not "circle,"' but that's what she says."

I was slipping on my sandals now, which was not easy to do with my arms folded in front of my breasts.

"I have to go," I said.

Darius sat up. "If you are going, then I am going," he

said, and he put on his shoes.

I hurried out into the parking lot ahead of him.

"Darius," I called back to him over my shoulder as he followed me to my car. "What was that about?"

"I like to be having interesting dates with you," he said. "Firsts."

Now we were standing by my car, facing each other.

I put my hand on the door handle. "Well, it is not interesting to bump into people from work," I said. "Goodbye."

He reached to open the door for me, but I pushed his hand away. I got in my car, slammed the door and drove off, singing "I've Been Working on the Railroad" at the top of my lungs. Behind me, I could see Darius through the rearview mirror, standing there, smiling in the summer night.

When I got home, Kate's car was not there. I parked crookedly in the driveway and turned off the motor and finally was able to reach around and hook up my bra. I lurched back in the house and called to Kate as I raced up to my room and slammed my door, even though I knew I was alone.

I sat on my bed and pulled the letter from Colonial Gracious Homes out of its envelope and stared at it like it was a bad report card. I wondered if this was my punishment for once again getting involved with the wrong man.

Nick's father, Bill, had been a portrait painter, and he had seduced me by saying, "Your hands are as graceful as envelopes" the day we met in the art museum in Eugene, where I had a job as a guide the summer before my freshman year in college. It was only later that I realized he probably told every woman he bedded that her hands reminded him of some kind of office supply. He left town and some laundry in the washing machine when I told him I was pregnant that spring.

I tried to focus on the birthday festivities to calm my nerves. Mrs. Flax had not indicated whether she was bringing a "gentleman caller," as she referred to her lovers, to the party, but I had planned to give her my bedroom with the double bed just in case, although I did not like to give up Joe's old room. I had decided I could sleep in the guest room. I always felt like a guest with Mrs. Flax around, anyway. But with Kate and Irving in the extra room now, everything was confused.

I sat on my bed, staring at the Colonial Gracious Homes letter and wishing I were as brave and strong as Ida Lewis, who had been a lighthouse keeper in Rhode Island. I'd read about her while doing research on saints when I was a teenager. In 1854, after her father had a paralyzing stroke, Ida became the keeper of Lime Rock Light. Every weekday, regardless of weather, she rowed her three younger siblings one-third of a mile to and from school on the mainland, and she became famous for her many daring sea rescues. When I was fourteen, I was in the bell tower with Joe Peretti, and my sister Kate almost drowned. When Ida was fourteen, she was keeping watch in a lighthouse and already saving lives.

—⌂—

CHAPTER 8

"A woman is like mahogany:
the older she is, the better she is."

—Haitian Proverb

That night, holding slides up to the light of my bedside lamp instead of projecting them on the wall, I found a slide of a photograph I'd taken of two nuns dancing in the moonlight, a blurred image of two young women in black habits doing some kind of dosey doe. Looking at it, I could hear them laughing and the sound of horseshoes clanging on stakes. I used to watch them out behind the pond, and once I swear I saw them kiss.

When Nick was young, I danced when he was asleep. I danced in the kitchen in my underwear with the radio turned low. My dream was to slow-dance with Joe Peretti, but I never did.

A woman student I had in Oregon who had fled Ger-

many during World War II told me once about the parties she and her husband used to have. When it was their
baby's bedtime, she said, they would lay her down ten-
derly on soft towels in the dry bathtub and carefully tie
another towel and shower cap over the shower head and
faucet so no dancing reveler turned on the water by mis-
take. She told me this in private, wondering if she had
been a good mother.

Another student, a woman named Loretta who had
been married and divorced four times since coming to
the United States, told me about how she had survived
the war in Holland by hiding in a barn and eating only
chestnuts. She still had nightmares about it, she said.
She told me once that she used to hum songs and dance
to keep warm and talked in great detail about her teenage lover, Hans, who had beautiful shoulders, and how
they would secretly meet by a brook deep in the woods
in the last summer days of August.

"We rip our clothes off, both our clothes, very fast,
and then make love many times, rolling," she said.
"One time was the most romantic. There were different
squash growing. Hans used this to make me excited. I
was very excited. Very."

I looked at one other slide that night, of the bell tower in the convent, and thought about how I would press
my cheek to the smooth stone when I snuck in to spy
on Joe Peretti, imagining I was pressing my cheek to
his loins. Now that the bell was gone and the tower con-
tained cable equipment, it did not have the same allure.

With Joe, there were what Kate used to call "chemicals." That night in the tower, he had pulled off his sweater and shirt and I had breathed in his warm chest. I was kissing his arms when he took off my underwear. He slid inside me and I held on tight as he filled me up. I thought I'd lost my breath forever, as if a great bird had fallen from my feet, and I was a virgin no more.

I often think that if Kate had not almost died the night Joe and I were half naked in the bell tower, he would not have left town, driving off in his brown Ford wearing a black suit and Indian moccasins, driving off to live with his sisters in Apalachicola.

CHAPTER 9

"Call on God, but row away
from the rocks."

—Indian Proverb

The next morning I awoke in a stupor at 5:30 A.M. with the sun. It was time to visit Lou Landsky at his shoe store. I made my way downstairs, holding onto the railing, like the whole house was swaying. I lurched out to the backyard where I did my tai chi, trying to calm myself as a row of sparrows landed on the clothesline like a tiny audience. I did my routine three times, and then I bowed to the sparrows.

I bent my head and made my way through the woods and stared at the condominiums. I could taste the butter cookies Mother Superior had served when I had visited her in her small cottage where one of the condominiums now stood, hoping she could help me figure out what to do about Joe Peretti. That was the day she had also confessed how scared she'd been when she joined the convent. Then she had talked on and on in a rambling way about how wonderful some man was, but this time I knew she wasn't talking about her brother. At first I thought she was talking about a priest, but then she mentioned the name Lou and I realized she was talking about Lou Landsky. She had fallen in love with him after coming to Grove to join the convent, she said, and had written him hundreds of letters over the years but had never mailed them. Instead, she had burned them in the fireplace in her cottage, even in the summertime.

I didn't know any of this the day she had come into Lou's shoe store with a young nun and sat down next to me and Kate to buy new nun shoes. I thought about that day a lot later and wondered what it had been like for her to sit there with Kate and me on one side and a young nun on the other and Lou holding her foot.

I don't know if she thought telling me about Lou would help me with Joe Peretti, but it didn't.

After my walk in the woods, I returned home to straighten up my room, Joe's old room, where Mrs. Flax would be staying when she arrived, if Mrs. Flax showed up. Kate and I would just have to share the guest room with little Irving.

Then I got myself together and drove into town and headed straight to the shoe store. I used to work there on Saturday mornings and many days after school, so I knew Lou would be there. He always got there early.

Lou Landsky was unique among Mrs. Flax's boy-
friends in that he was older than she was. She didn't call
him her "boyfriend," however. She never used that word
and disliked it when I did. I could just hear her saying,
"Charlotte, for God's sakes!"

I stood outside Lou's store for a moment, gazing at
the window display. It seemed that news of Colonial Gracious Homes' plan to kick me out of 4 Harvest Road had
already begun to spread. Along with a messy display of
running shoes, there was a big cardboard cutout of what
looked like a teenager's bed in Lou's window, with a sign
under it written in red magic marker: Colonial Gracious
Homes Should Be More Gracious!

I was touched. I doubted that more than a few people
would know what he was talking about, but still.

I walked up the wooden steps and pushed open the
door, and the tiny bells above the inside of the door jangled as they always did. The store still smelled of shoe
polish and lemon drops.

There were no nuns in the musty shop buying nun
shoes this time, and there was no cardboard portrait
of Buster Brown and his dog. But the window was still
bordered with little sailing flags Lou had made and in-
scribed with the same old slogan: "Sail to a sale! Sail to
a sale!" When I worked in the store, I used to put those
little flags in the shoes on the inside display racks.

Now, there was a young woman from somewhere
in Eastern Europe at the counter, stapling receipts together. She was a former student of mine, but I couldn't

remember her name.

"Hello," I said. "Is Mr. Landsky in?"

"Good afternoon, Mrs. Charlotte," she said, smiling and reaching to shake my hand as I surveyed the store. It was basically the same. I could hear the sounds of a radio tuned to a baseball game coming from the back room. That's where you could always find Lou when he wasn't busy with customers, surrounded by boxes of shoes, listening to a ball game on the radio. Mrs. Flax used to say, "I personally don't like baseball, but I couldn't like a *man* who doesn't like baseball."

Lou would have been a good stepfather. It would have been good for me and Kate if Mrs. Flax had married him, and even good for Nick to have grown up with a grandfather he knew.

"Mr. Landsky went to the dentist," the young woman said, going back to her stapling.

I picked up a light blue running shoe with a "Sail to a sale!" flag in it and examined it as I waited for her to say more. But she just kept stapling, so I put the shoe back down and turned and walked out the door. The bell jangled again as I left and headed across the street to Luscious Table Caterers.

You had to be buzzed into this shop. The proprietor, a young woman in her twenties named Celeste, was behind the counter, and she seemed to hesitate for a moment when she saw me. I touched my hair, thinking it must look a little wild, but then she buzzed, and I almost fell into the store.

The store used to be a second-hand book shop, but

there was no musty smell of old books left over from the previous tenant. A bayberry candle scented the air.

Celeste was dressed in gray linen slacks and top and gold flats. Her hair and makeup were perfect. She surveyed my frazzled hair and wrinkled clothes and sighed.

"And how may I help you today?" she asked coolly.

I wanted to tell her that, when I was her age, I didn't need makeup or fancy clothes or gold shoes for men to look at me, they always looked at me, but I refrained. Instead, I said that my good friend Carrie Giordano had told me that Celeste had said she might be able to give me a discount on catering Mrs. Flax's party and that I should ask Celeste about it. Carrie knows everyone in Grove, and her name carries weight.

"Oh, yes," Celeste said. "I was waiting for another booking to confirm. We do have a wedding at Cooks earlier that same day, and sometimes when we have two events at the same venue, if both clients order the same menu, we can prepare additional portions at less cost and pass the savings along." She paused. "We've done that," she said, giving me a slightly disapproving look, "in certain cases."

"That would be great!" I said. I wanted to ask her, "Is it true your mother was a nun?" But, instead, I asked her what the menu was.

"Lasagna and salad," she said. "Of course, we wouldn't supply the birthday cake."

"Of course not," I said. I wanted to ask if there had been a pair of nun shoes in the back of her mother's closet when she was growing up. "This sounds good," I said.

"I'll call you soon. Thank you very much."

I went back to Lou's store and left a note for him with my former student:

> Dear Lou,
> Hope you're well. It's Mrs. Flax's birthday in a few weeks, and I'm having a party at Cooks. I'd love you to be there. September 2nd at 7 P.M.

I added my phone number, and, just as I was leaving, Lou appeared from the back of the store—stouter, grayer, but with the same playful eyes—with one hand stuck in a scuffed, brown men's oxford shoe. He wore khakis stained with shoe polish and a red checked cotton shirt. "Shahlotte! Shahlotte Rose!" he boomed in his Boston accent. He was the only person who ever used my middle name, and I never minded. I let him embrace me, with that shoe banging into my back, and for a moment I had yearnings the way Mrs. Flax must have had, even though he was almost eighty now.

"What's cookin,' good lookin'?" he boomed again, grinning. "Carrie told me about them trying to kick you out. Maybe you should start a petition. I'll sign it." Lou ripped a piece of paper from a big notebook on the counter and wrote his name on the first line. "Here you go, kiddo," he said, handing the paper to me.

"Thank you," I said. "And thanks for the sign in the window. I'm going to fight it. My first fight. Any advice?"

"I shouldn't let those condo people buy my shoes," Lou muttered.

"Wish you could do that," I sighed. "It's a nice

thought, anyway. Lou, Mrs. Flax is coming to town."

He looked surprised, then wistful, and then he beamed. "She coming solo?" he asked.

"Far as I know. It's her sixtieth birthday, and I'm giving her a party at Cooks on Labor Day," I said, nodding to the note on the counter. "Would you like to come?"

"Wouldn't miss it, wouldn't miss it," he said, smiling and shaking his head.

Lou has children and grandchildren who live far away. When we lived in Grove, he went to visit them for Thanksgiving and came back sadder than when he left.

We hugged again, and I started to leave.

"Shahlotte," he said, like there was something else he wanted to say. I hesitated. "I don't know how to say this," said Lou, picking up the scuffed brown oxford and sliding it back on his hand like a baseball glove. "Needs stitching," he said, examining the shoe.

I nodded, not knowing what he was getting at.

"Shahlotte," he repeated, still looking at the shoe. "There's been some talk in town. About the young man at the college."

At that I froze.

"I should go, Lou," I said, folding the sheet of notebook paper he had signed and putting it in my bag. "I hope you can come to the party."

"I care about you, Shahlotte," he said as I hurried out the front door. "I really do."

—⌂—

CHAPTER 10

"Ashamed of what she sees in the daytime
the Sun sets with a blush."

—Armenian Proverb

did not respond to the letter from Colonial Gracious
Homes. In fact, when I got back from visiting Lou, I
threw the letter in the outside garbage can. But later
that night, when I knew the Colonial Gracious Homes
office would be closed, I dialed the number and got an
answering machine.

"Welcome to Colonial Gracious Homes," an artificial-
ly gracious recorded female voice said. "You have called
during non-office hours. We are happy to serve you by
phone or in person Monday through Friday, nine a.m. to
five p.m., Saturday, ten a.m. to four p.m., and Sunday,
eleven a.m. to three p.m. Please leave a message includ-
ing your name and a phone number where you can be

reached, and we will return your call as soon as possible. If you are calling about one of our 32 other communities nationwide, please call our central office at 214-754-2323 or write to Colonial Gracious Homes, Post Office Box 2323, Dallas, Texas, 75201. Thank you for your call."

The letter I had received hadn't said anything about other communities or offices in Texas. That's when I realized I wasn't just dealing with a local developer who wanted to build more condominiums next door. Colonial Gracious Homes was a national corporation. Fighting to save Joe's house was going to be harder than I thought.

The next day, Sunday, I went to the library. The librarian, old Miss Flory George, who wore a white lab coat stained with ink over her clothes, did not exactly welcome me, but I held my head high as I walked past her to the stacks. I ran my hands along the spines of the books to comfort myself as I walked up and down the rows.

Finally, I found a section, actually half a shelf, labeled "Local History and Lore." My hand stopped on a thin book with a cracked leather binding. I could just make out the words "Historic" and "Grove" on the spine. I pulled it off the shelf. The full title was *Historic Homes of Grove*. I opened it slowly. The pages were thick and yellowed, with line drawings of buildings and houses. I sat in the corner on a wooden step stool, gently holding the book in my lap, turning the fragile pages one by one, hoping to find a way to save my home.

I read in that book that the Protectors of the Blessed

Souls Convent had been built in 1899, and my house, the Perettis' house, had been built in 1928. The buildings weren't technically historical landmarks. If they had been, Colonial Gracious Homes wouldn't have been able to build the condominiums in the first place. But there was history there. It seemed that my beloved home had been a guest house, where parents, some bereft, some proud, stayed for a night or two or three when they delivered their dear daughters to a life of cold showers and prayer. I could see them pacing on my porch, wiping away their tears, wondering how these teenage girls, still in the first throes of young womanhood, who had had crushes on boys who drove roadsters, could decide they wanted to take the veil and become married to Christ.

I secretly had hoped to find evidence that 4 Harvest Road had been a stop on the Underground Railroad, so I'd have a reason to try to get it declared a historical landmark, but the house had been built long after the Civil War, and learning that it had been a way station for parents of nuns-to-be was as far as I got.

I sat in the library, remembering how much I had yearned to join the Protectors of the Blessed Souls when I was fourteen, and, for a moment, I had the urge to join a convent again. I closed the book and put it back on the shelf.

Climbing the porch steps, I realized I hadn't checked the mail the day before. I reached into the mailbox and pulled out a PennySaver flyer and a small envelope postmarked from Eugene, Oregon, sent first to my old address there and then forwarded. The envelope was the size of a child's thank-you note. There was no return address, but I recognized the cardiologist's handwriting from all the prescriptions he had written for Nick and the charts on his desk that we always had to move aside when we met in his office.

I sat on the porch swing and opened the letter slowly.

Dear Charlotte,

I miss our times. Nobody understands me the way you do. I plan to be on the East Coast for a conference around Thanksgiving.

I'll give you a call.

There was no signature.

I crumpled the note and threw it in the outside garbage can.

When I was in elementary school in Irvine, California, I once watched girls play jump rope during recess on a hot September playground, but I was afraid to jump in myself. I wasn't sure how. A boy in horn-rimmed glasses walked up to me and held a conch shell to my ear. He said I'd hear the ocean, but I knew even then that all I was hearing was the sounds inside my own head.

It wasn't until I got the Colonial Gracious Homes letter that I understood I would finally have to jump in, although I had no idea what I was jumping into.

I stayed up late that night writing a letter to the *Grove Sentinel*.

I wrote about living in Grove when I was fourteen

and choosing to return. I wrote about the history of the convent and the Peretti house and how evicting hard-working residents of modest means to turn the house into an office for a walled condo community was not the gracious thing for Colonial Gracious Homes to do. I was quite eloquent. At midnight, I drove into town in my nightgown and put my letter in the mailbox outside the post office.

CHAPTER 11

"Act in the valley so that you need not fear
those who stand on the hill."

—Danish Proverb

I made two dozen sugar-cinnamon cookies for class the
next day to add to the cookies some of the students
had volunteered to bring in after writing about their
favorite childhood desserts. A Latvian man brought in
bowknot cookies, a Thai woman made coconut cookies
and an elderly Estonian man brought in oatmeal cookies
he said his wife had made. Darius was there, looking as
handsome as ever, sitting in the front row, but not showing any hint to me or anyone else that we had touched
each other's nakedness.

We set out all the cookies on my desk like it was a
kitchen counter, and Darius brushed up against my back
as he reached to take two of my sugar cookies, which

made me almost faint. He had brought Hawaiian Punch and paper cups and poured drinks for everybody like a professional bartender, and I was in an altered state.

I tried to steer the conversation to a discussion of pronouns as we all stood around eating cookies, with crumbs on our faces and the fronts of our clothes. But suddenly the woman whose father had been beheaded in Afghanistan and the elderly man from Estonia were having a heated argument—in English, although I could not understand what they were saying. And then, just as I was starting to fantasize about paying another visit to Darius's house, I realized he had gone. I stayed with the other students, forcing myself not to run after him, listening intently to the woman from Afghanistan argue with the man from Estonia.

After the students had all left, I swept the crumbs off my desk and pressed the large can of Hawaiian Punch to my lips, thinking of Darius. I knew I was becoming addicted, as I had with the cardiologist, so I resisted the impulse to drive to Darius's house after class and forced myself to drive to the library to read more about the history of Grove.

I parked in the library parking lot and stared at myself in the rearview mirror. I had an unhinged look in my eyes again. I tried to do my tai chi breathing as I walked up the library steps, but it was hard to concentrate.

The library was empty except for a few sweaty kids doing book reports on their summer reading assignments and one harried-looking woman being softly scolded by Miss Flory George for returning her books late. I walked back to the shelf on local history and lore, pulled another old volume off the shelf and sat on the wood stool in the corner, as if I were a truant child. I read in this book that a priest from a neighboring parish had stood on the porch at 4 Harvest Road and blessed my house when it was first built, and that when Pope Paul VI celebrated Mass at Yankee Stadium during his one-day visit to the United States on October 4, 1965, some of the nuns who were still at the convent drove in their nun car all the way to the Bronx to see him. There was a photograph in the book that had appeared in the *Grove Sentinel* of the four of them screaming and weeping like they were at a Beatles concert.

When I got home, there was another postcard in the mailbox from Mrs. Flax, a black-and-white photo of what must have been one of the first filling stations, because it showed a horse and buggy parked right next to an early Ford. Mrs. Flax had scrawled across the back, *Countdown to my eighteenth birthday party! I love cheese-ball pick-me-ups!*

Kate and Irving were not home. The house was a mess. There were bits of Play-Doh and chewed-up stick all over the rug. I ran upstairs, showered and shaved my legs, changed into clean underwear and put on a simple black cotton dress. I sprayed rose perfume behind my knees and drove out of Grove, out onto the New England summer roads, north to where Darius lived, two towns away.

Turning into his driveway, I looked in the rearview mirror to smooth my eyebrows, then slammed on the brakes to avoid hitting the car already parked in front of me. It was a green 1987 Honda Civic. Kate's car. Kate was at Darius's house.

It took me a few moments to absorb what I was seeing. Then I wanted to ram her goddamned Honda Civic at full speed. Instead, I slowly backed out of the driveway, feeling a twisting in my stomach. My chi was not in a calm and balanced state the way it was supposed to be. I slowly, slowly drove away, gripping the steering wheel tight. When I got to the main road, I started screaming. Next thing I knew, I was behind a very big, slow truck with red arrows painted on the left and right bumpers, one pointing up, one pointing down. The one pointing up said read "Heaven," and the one pointing down read "Hell."

When I returned home, I fell into bed with my clothes on and pounded my pillow like a child.

At 10:30 that night, the phone rang just as I was drifting off. It was Kate, jangling my soul. The moment I heard her voice, I had the same stabbing feeling I'd had when Nick's father, Bill, had explained that he didn't believe humans were naturally monogamous. Even so, I had called Bill's father in Wyoming after Bill left and said quietly, "I thought Bill and I were going to get married," as if he would talk sense into his son. But he just said in his western drawl, "Yep, you kids might could have, you might could have. I'd a thought you would."

I wanted to hang up on Kate, but I didn't. She was breathing heavily. What if she was in trouble?

"I need some advice about your student Darius," she whispered conspiratorially, not sounding in any kind of trouble at all, except the usual Kate kind.

"My advice is, stay away from my—my student," I spat.

I heard Kate take a quick breath. "Ohmygod. He's your boyfriend!" She made a soft sound, like a little laugh. "Charlotte, I didn't know. Really. I ran into him yesterday in front of the tomato sauces at that little gourmet place in town. We started talking, and I told him how Mrs. Peretti used to make her own sauce, and then I mentioned my barbecue sauce, and he said he'd like to try it, and I asked if he had a grill and.... Oh, Charlotte, you know men just want to get it wet."

At that I slammed down the phone. It rang again, but I didn't answer. Not only did I not love Darius. Right then, I didn't even like the man. Or Kate. I stared out my bedroom window at the maple trees blowing in the night summer breeze and cursed my sister. I missed the old Kate. The sister I'd had when she and Mrs. Flax and I had all lived in this house together. The sister I almost lost while Joe and I were in the bell tower.

I went down to the kitchen and pulled a half-eaten pint of pistachio ice cream out of the freezer. It was hard as a rock. I put it down on the kitchen table and sat down with a spoon, waiting for it to soften, waiting for the phone to ring again.

I missed the old refrigerator, too. The freezer compartment never closed properly and didn't freeze ice cream so hard and had to be defrosted about once a month. I'd eat all the ice cream left in the freezer, then open the compartment and refrigerator door and wait for the thick layers of frost and ice to melt. I'd sit at this very table for hours, waiting to hear the sound of ice cracking and falling. I loved that sound. Waiting for Kate to call back was like waiting for that ice to fall.

I was back in bed, drifting in and out of sleep when I heard Kate pull into the driveway. I looked at the clock. It was three-thirty a.m. I jumped out of bed, threw on a robe, staggered down to the kitchen and flicked on the light just as Kate came in carrying Irving, who was sound asleep on her chest.

She slumped down in a chair, still holding Irving, her hair and clothes disheveled, gave me a half smile and whispered over Irving's head, "He's a very attractive man. What could I do?"

She might as well have been saying that she ran into a big sale on paper towels and how could she resist?

It was at this point that I wondered where Irving had been while Kate and Darius had frolicked, but I did not ask. I stood there in my bathrobe with my arms folded across my chest and fumed. If Kate hadn't had Irving in her arms, I would have slapped her.

"He has such an interesting profession," Kate said. "I mean, who studies firsts? He's just a very interesting man, don't you think?" She put her hands on Irving's head and looked up at me, serene as the Virgin Mary.

I wheeled around and started to stomp out of the kitchen, but I stopped, turned back, took a step toward her and glared down at her.

"Kate Flax," I said slowly, "don't you ever, ever touch one of my men again," at which point Irving woke up and started crying.

We both tried to soothe Irving back to sleep, but he continued to wail. I gave up trying to comfort him and stomped up the stairs to my room and slammed the door.

The first year after my grandmother died, there was an exquisiteness to my sorrow, like black ice glittering on a hidden pond. "After great pain, a formal feeling comes," wrote Emily Dickinson. For me, the second year after my grandmother's death marked the beginning of my return to the real world. The first year was like the first night camping out alone—uncomfortable and a little frightening but breathtaking to see the night sky, to feel the extreme solitude. The second year was like camping out forever. I had had enough. I did not want to be camping out anymore.

After I heard Kate climb the stairs and shut the door to her room, and after Irving stopped crying and seemed to settle back into sleep, I went and stood outside their door with my fists clenched. I wanted to pound on the door, break it down, storm in and scream at Kate, but I couldn't bear to wake little Irving.

Instead, I went into the bathroom, rummaged through the medicine cabinet for an old tube of bright pink lipstick, closed the cabinet and wrote on the mirror in large pink letters, "Kate, Please Leave."

I must have slept soundly after that, because I didn't wake up until past ten, and when I did, the house was quiet. I went downstairs and found a note on the kitchen table:

> *Need to get away for a while.*
> *Be back for the party.*
> *Love, Kate and Irving*

CHAPTER 12

"A girl without a needle is like
a cat without a claw."

—Estonian Proverb

marched through the next two days with shaking
hands, gorging on blueberry sandwiches.

I did not drive out to Darius's house, although I did
pass him on the road once, driving the other way in his
dark red SUV, and it crossed my mind to accidentally
crash my faded yellow Mazda into his car. At least, I
believed it was his car, although, in my shaken state, I
could not be sure. As angry as I was with Kate, I missed
my sister and that stick-eating boy. Rationality is not my
middle name.

The first thing I did the day after Kate left was clean
the lipstick off the bathroom mirror. The second thing I
did was call Carrie.

Carrie is good in emergencies. Maybe she had to learn how to be when her son, Kenneth, was little, though I never, ever heard her complain about having to take care of him. She was the first person who came by to comfort us after John F. Kennedy was killed. I was in history class when the news spread through Grove High. Our teacher, Mr. Crain, was standing at the blackboard, shuffling baseball cards, about to choose two students to engage in an imaginary debate between Louis IV and Franklin Delano Roosevelt when his wife, who was the guidance counselor and later ran off with Kate's swim coach, poked her crew-cut head in the door. "The President has been shot," she said. "The President is dead."

School let out immediately, and I ran home, barely breathing. Mrs. Flax and Kate were sitting on the couch watching TV. Mrs. Flax was crying, and Kate was crying because Mrs. Flax was crying, and everybody on TV was crying, but my face was dry as paper. While I was standing in front of the TV, switching channels, someone knocked at the door. When I opened it, there was Carrie, who was still an Avon Lady then, with her plastic cosmetics case full of the newest sample lipsticks and perfumes.

"Hi, honey," she said. "You okay?" I nodded, and opened the door wider for her to come in. "It's a sad day, a very sad day," she said, sitting down next to Mrs. Flax and putting an arm around her. "He had such beautiful hair." She looked at me. "And you have beautiful eyes, Charlotte. Remember that. Just like Elizabeth Taylor."

That was the beginning of our friendship. After that,

whenever Carrie thought I looked upset about something, she'd say, "If you ever want to talk...." That's all. Sometimes I took her up on the offer, sometimes I didn't. But it was good just to know she was there.

I knew talking to Carrie would help me sort out my feelings, but it didn't matter if I couldn't reach her, and she did not pick up her phone when I called, so I left a message saying I needed to talk. Then I lay back down on my bed and imagined my sister and Darius making love in his entryway, with baby Irving marching around that house with a stick, and I wondered how many times Kate and Darius had been together.

I didn't hear back from Carrie that day and I couldn't sleep again that night. I counted how often Darius and I had been together and tried counting other things, like sheep, and then I thought of what Joe Peretti had told me about Hannibal as we were driving around in the school bus one day after he'd dropped off all the other kids. Joe said that Hannibal had crossed the Alps from Spain into Italy in 218 B.C. with 50,000 infantry, 9,000 cavalry and 37 elephants. I never forgot those numbers. They've stayed with me ever since. I chant them like a mantra to calm my fraying nerves when I have trouble sleeping and usually drift off imagining elephants plodding through a snowstorm in the Alps.

Counting elephants didn't soothe me this time, though. I did my tai chi and still I could not sleep. So I decided to look at slides. I keep the slides organized and labeled in a series of shoeboxes, and I keep the projector covered with a piece of old blue velvet, like a sacred relic. I don't look at dozens of slides at a time. Only a few. I like to savor them. That night, I decided I would look at three:

Slide 1. *Sioux Falls, Kate and Charlotte Ice Skating, Holding Hands.* When we were living in South Dakota, Mrs. Flax decided to create an ice-skating rink in our backyard. Kate and I built snow walls in a crooked rectangle around the whole yard. Then Mrs. Flax called the local volunteer fire department, which included the grocer, the barber, the candy store man, all men she knew, and they came out one night with a fire hose and sprayed water on the frozen ground. One of them, the candy store man, offered to stay and hook up an outdoor light. We couldn't skate that night because the water needed to freeze first, and there was a full moon, so we did not really need the light, but the next morning the ice was frozen, and Kate and I went out and slid around in our shoes before school, and we found the candy store man's scarf in the driveway when we got home.

Slide 2. *Eugene, Pastor Jim in front of museum.* I met Jim while I was working as a guide at the art museum. He was a Lutheran minister, but he didn't look like one. I smiled at the picture of him, standing outside the museum, hands in his jacket pockets, squinting into the sun with his curly brown hair grazing the top of his collar. He looked like a hippie, except for his white collar. He had a ham sandwich wrapped in a paper towel in his left pocket. I know this because we shared it afterward on a bench. He told me as we ate that French sailors never allow rabbits aboard their ships and never even say the word "lapin," which means rabbit, during a voyage because they believe rabbits bring bad luck. He said the superstition got started in the seventeenth century when sailors brought live rabbits aboard as food, but before the cute little rabbits could all be cooked and eaten, they would gnaw through the wooden hulls and send the boats to the bottom of the sea.

Slide 3. *Des Moines, Kate's Rocks.* Kate used to collect rocks and kept her precious collection in a Buster Brown shoebox. One day, when we were living in Des Moines, I came home from school and Mrs. Flax was in bed. "I'm having a spell," she said, like she was a southern belle. That was all she said. She stayed in bed for a week and wore a shower cap at night because we had bats in that house. I took charge of cooking for Kate and me and getting us both to school. After school, we would go into the yard with a hammer and chip pieces of mica from the rocks in the garden behind the house. We'd hold the mica chips up to the sun and watch them sparkle, then add them to Kate's box. I carried that box around with us for years, wrapping it up carefully along with Kate's swim trophies every time we moved. I don't remember how it disappeared.

I put the slides back in the shoebox and put the projector away. Still I could not sleep, so I dragged out my sewing basket. I went through the clothes in the front of my closet until I found an old, pale green, shirtwaist dress that was missing a button on the sleeve. Then I went into the back of the closet, where I kept my grandfather's old shirts, pulled one out and carefully snipped a button off the cuff. Then I sat on my bed and sewed my grandfather's button onto what Nick used to call my "lots of buttons dress."

I was up the entire night. It was getting light when I finished sewing, so I took a shower and started getting ready for school. My stomach was twisting again. I didn't know if I was hoping Darius would be in class or if I was hoping he wouldn't. I was buttoning up the front of the green dress when the phone rang. I picked it up on the second ring, hoping it would be Carrie. It was not Carrie.

"Good morning," a male voice said politely. "May I speak with Charlotte Flax?" For a moment, I had the crazy thought that it was my father calling from England, but it didn't sound like a long-distance connection. "Good morning," the man repeated. "Is this Miss Flax?"

"Who's calling?" I asked.

"My name is Charles Winterson. I'm calling from Colonial Gracious Homes."

"Colonial Gracious Homes where?" I asked. He did not seem to have a Texas accent.

"Grove office," he said.

I did as many tai chi breaths as I could before responding. "Good morning," I said firmly. "You have no right to take away my home."

"That's what I'm calling about, Miss Flax," Mr. Winterson said. "You haven't responded to our letter, but we saw your letter in the paper today, so we thought we would reach out to you. Miss Flax, please be assured that we have no intention of taking away anything that belongs to you. But, as I'm sure you are aware, you are not the owner of the property at 4 Harvest Road. You are a tenant. Our tenant, to be precise. We are not trying to take away any of your possessions. We are simply asking you to relocate, which it is within our rights as the owners of the property to do. Surely, 4 Harvest Road is not the only house available for rental in the area. There are many other lovely locations in Grove. And, of course, we will soon have additional condominiums available for purchase in our expanding Grove community. Perhaps you would be interested in one of our units?"

"No. No, thank you," I murmured.

"Well, you don't have to decide immediately," he said formally. "You have until the first of December. Surely, you will be able to find something suitable by then. After all, you're not new in town, are you?"

"No," I said softly. "No, I'm not."

CHAPTER 13

"If you don't want anybody
to know, don't do it."

—Chinese Proverb

I hung up the phone, made myself a banana sandwich and went out to the porch to pick up the *Grove Sentinel*. I sat on the swing, eating the sandwich with one hand and leafing through the paper with the other. The front page had stories about oil well fires that were still burning in Kuwait and a new mall that was opening soon outside of town. I turned to Letters to the Editor, and there it was, my letter, with the title "Gracious Move?"

The editors had made one change. They had taken out the line, "I'll leave over my dead body." The rest of the letter was just as I had written it. It was longer than I remembered, but I thought it was quite good. It traced the convent's history and told about how the house at

4 Harvest Road had once been a guesthouse for families dropping their daughters off to begin their holy and celibate lives. It said a little about the Perettis, who had lived their whole lives in Grove and had once owned the gas station and bar, and it ended with my story of deciding to come back to live in Grove because it was such a wonderful and welcoming place and how heartless it was for Colonial Gracious Homes to make me move now, when I was already a grandmother, for goodness sake. It was the only letter the paper ran that day, so it was hard to miss.

Darius did not show up for class that day, and I kept glancing at the door as if he would magically appear. Two of my students mentioned that they had seen my letter in the paper. A Korean man sitting in the front row raised his hand and said he hoped I could stay in my "homeland." Then he leaned forward in his seat, waved for me to lean closer, like he was going to tell me a secret, and whispered, "Mr. Darius has dropped on the college." I nodded, as if to thank him for that helpful piece of information and tried to look unfazed. So that was that. I would not be seeing Darius at Grove Community College anymore.

It was for the best, I knew. It would be best if I never saw him again anywhere. I mulled that over. I still knew where he lived. Could I stay away? Then a woman from

Peru raised her hand and said, "You are brave," which nobody had ever said to me before in my life.

I did not go home after class. Instead, I drove directly to Carrie's house. Some families in Grove whose loved ones had returned from the Gulf War had removed the yellow ribbons from around the trees in front of their houses, but with Carrie and Tim's son, Kenneth, still over there, the yellow ribbons tied to the slender birches and maples along their driveway remained.

Tim had rigged a bunch of hoses on the flat roof of their modern, glass-windowed house to cool things down during the hot summer months, even though it wasted water. I parked next to Carrie's van, smoothed my hair and checked my expression in the rearview mirror, trying to look less deranged. As I was doing this, Carrie came out the front door and dashed through the mini-waterfall that was streaming down off her roof.

"Come on in here, Miss Charlotte," she said, smiling and waving me inside. "I hear you have a real estate problem."

Carrie looked quite striking with her gray hair, wearing an olive green sweatshirt and pants. I walked ahead of her into the house, letting myself get a little wet from the waterfall, looking for salvation from the heat and my sins.

"I don't want to move," I moaned, collapsing on her orange couch and fanning myself with my hand.

Carrie shook her head. "I'll go make some iced Chai tea," she said.

I slumped deeper into her couch and thought of Nick's father, Bill, and what it would have been like if we had stayed together. Before I got pregnant with Nick, Bill and I had been very close. Or perhaps I just liked to think that.

I know exactly when and where we created Nick. It was on the porch in Eugene, just after midnight in early September of 1967, at the beginning of my freshman year in college. It was a warm night, so we took our pillows and sheets out on the porch, put the blankets down for padding and kept trying to get comfortable on the wood planks. We were laughing, and then Bill said we'd be cooler if we took off our nightclothes. I did a little striptease in the dark, and he kept whispering, "I can't see you, I can't see you" while reaching for me.

Everything changed that night, just as it did the night my grandmother died and the day Nick was born. Something shifted and divided into before and after, after and before. I didn't know what the shift was that night or what the "after" would be. I just knew it had begun.

"You're a grown woman," Carrie said, sitting next to me on the orange couch and handing me the glass of iced Chai tea. "You have to start learning to accept loss." She paused. "I heard about you and some divorced student."

At that I froze.

"We'll find you a cheaper place to live," Carrie continued when I didn't respond, "and you can start selling some of my natural products. You need to be like a starfish. If they lose an arm, they grow it back."

I set my glass down on the coffee table and put my head in my hands. Carrie started massaging my shoulders.

"I don't love him," I said. "I mean, now my sister is after the guy." I couldn't bring myself to tell Carrie that Kate had already caught him, but she did not seem surprised by what I said about Kate. Grove was a very small town.

Carrie patted my shoulder, stood up to stretch and remained standing, balanced on one foot like a crane. "Look," she said, "you can get through this. And you never know how things will turn out. My father survived the Great Hurricane of 1938. All the power went out. Whole houses were floating away. The flooding was so bad on Main Street that people were escaping in boats." Carrie put her hands on her hips. "My father was working as a caddie at the golf club with his best friend, James Eady, when the hurricane hit. They usually rode home on the streetcar with two young waitresses. The only thing the four of them could think to do when the water started rushing in was climb a big, sturdy sugar maple on the edge of the golf course. While they were up in that tree, those two boys started kissing those two girls. None of them had ever kissed or been kissed before, but they all figured that if they were going to die, they wanted to get kissed first. Well, one of those girls was my mother."

"And what's your point?" I said, sulking. "You want me to go up a tree and kiss somebody?"

Carrie lowered her leg.

"My point is," said Carrie, "one door opens and another one opens, or a window opens or whatever that expression is."

I stared at my hands.

"Look at your hands," Carrie said, frowning. "They're chapped. You have to keep your hands soft. That's very important." She went into the kitchen again and came back with a jar of avocado cream. She pulled off the lid, scooped out a handful of green grease and began smoothing it onto my hands. "Here," she said, handing me the jar. "Go home, use this and then get some sleep."

I drove home, holding the steering wheel with my greasy hands. I thought that possibly I could move to Rochester, not in with my son and daughter-in-law and the twins, but near them. Maybe that would be the window opening or the door opening, or at least a place to hang my hat.

—⌂—

CHAPTER 14

"The house does not rest upon
the ground, but upon a woman."

—Mexican Proverb

I called Nick at his office the next morning, hoping for guidance.

"Good morning, Mother," he said cheerfully. I could just see him swiveling around in his chair, and then I pictured him spinning around in the tire swing on the playground when he was a little boy.

Each time I see Nick, I want to put my ear to his heart. I had visited him at his office in Rochester once, driving straight there from the airport, and had refrained from kissing him on the cheek or putting my ear to his heart in front of his colleagues. His hair had been shaggy, and he had always had impish eyes. As my grandmother would have said, "The wildest creature in the barnyard is a human boy." There were big Kodacolor pictures of pandas and elephants lining the hallways, but Nick preferred black-and-white photography. On his desk was a black-and-white photo of the twins sleeping head-to-head in a single crib, one of Regina at the beach with her hands in the air and one of Nick leaping off a cliff in that ridiculous winged hang-glider contraption.

"Hi, honey, how are you and Regina and the girls?" I asked, doing my special tai chi breathing, trying to sound calm so he wouldn't hear that I was upset.

"Lisa and Becky are in a competition to see who can drink their bottles the fastest," he said, laughing. "How are you? Everything okay? You just called last week. Is the party still on?"

"Oh, yes, of course. Can't forget sixty," I said, doing a few more tai chi breaths. "They want me to move," I finally blurted.

"Who?" Nick asked, sounding a little distracted. I pictured him swiveling the other way in his chair. "Why?"

"The convent—I mean, the condominium developers. They're expanding. They want the house back."

"When?" Nick asked, sounding more attentive now.

"Not until December. I'm trying to fight it."

I felt like I was going to cry, and it was at that moment that I realized I could not move to Rochester. I would drive Nick crazy, and I would go crazy living there.

"Mom?" Nick said softly. "Are you there?" I couldn't answer. "I'm sorry, Mom," he said. Even though he had never been to the Grove house, he knew how much it meant to me.

"We'll figure it out," I said, and then I heard someone talking to him in his office.

"We'll figure it out," he repeated. "I have to go now, but we'll figure it out."

"Thanks, sweetie," I said. "I know we will." And then we both hung up.

Nick was a good son. He'd always put up with the Flax women. One winter night in Eugene, when Nick was eight, he was upstairs in his room, playing with his array of toy vehicles, and I was heating Campbell's tomato soup and making grilled-cheese sandwiches for dinner when the phone rang.

"I need help," Kate said before I even said hello. I hadn't seen or spoken to her in more than a year.

"I need to talk to you," she said. "I'm coming over."

"Where are you?"

"I'm at the Safeway, at the phone outside, where the carts are. I need help."

"I was just there. Are you okay?" I said, crooking the phone between my ear and shoulder as I turned the grilled-cheese sandwiches and stirred the soup. I knew that was a stupid question, but I repeated it. "Are you okay?"

"I know, I saw you there," said Kate. "Can I come over?"

"You were there? I didn't see you. Yeah, sure," I said hesitantly. "Are you alone?"

"I'll be over in a few minutes," Kate said and hung up.

I put down the spoon and went into the bathroom and stared at myself in the mirror. I'm not sure why I did that, probably just to see my own face and remind myself that I existed. My hair was pulled back in a ponytail, and my eyes looked darker than usual. I brushed my teeth and put on a tiny bit of rose lipstick, as if I were expecting a date, but ten minutes later, when Kate screeched into the driveway, I had already licked it off.

I peered out the window, and there she was, storming up the stairs wearing tight blue jeans and a fisherman's sweater, her long, curly red hair bouncing.

"I'm cold," she said as she hugged me fiercely at the door.

"Should I make a fire?" I offered.

Kate shook her head. "I'm not sure what to do with my life," she said, following me back into the kitchen.

"Well, you're good at a lot of things," I said lamely, turning off the heat under the soup and putting water on for tea.

It was beginning to snow, which was rare in Eugene.

"I like the snow," Kate said, looking out the window.

"You always did," I said.

"Let's take our tea out in the snow," Kate said.

"I thought you were cold," I said, pouring two mugs of mint tea.

I grabbed my coat and followed Kate out into the cold. We stood in our coats on the porch where Nick had been conceived, holding our hot tea and watching as the flakes fell, frosting the yard.

"I think I'd like to have a child," Kate said.

I almost laughed. I wanted to say, "Do you have any idea how hard it is to raise a child?" Instead, I turned and went back inside and let Kate dance around with the snowflakes. This was fourteen years before she turned up in Grove with a stick-eating boy.

I went upstairs to tell Nick that his Aunt Kate was here. He was kneeling by his bed, meticulously setting out rescue vehicles on his cowboy bedspread.

"I know a different word for penis," he said softly without looking up.

"Really, what's that?" I said, trying to convey no known human emotion.

"Family jewels," Nick said solemnly, looking up at me with innocent eyes.

"Where'd you learn that?"

"School."

"Your Aunt Kate is here."

He frowned. "Is she going to be crazy again?" he asked.

The last time Kate had visited us, she had gone out almost every evening, always dressed provocatively, and once Nick had seen her come back in the morning with her hair and clothes a mess as he was leaving for school.

I smiled and stroked his head. "Come down soon," I said. "Be polite. It's time for dinner."

Nick never had to share a room or my love and attention, which could have made him spoiled, but it didn't. Kate and I had always shared a room with bunk beds wherever we lived, but that didn't seem to guarantee us peace on earth. She always had the top bunk, and, in the days when she was a swimmer and as sweet as pie, I would climb up there with her and tell her made-up stories about our fathers to help her sleep.

When Kate started developing and stopped swimming, she stepped on my leg every time she climbed up to the top bunk. On nights when she snuck out, I'd climb up there and lay my head on her pillow, trying to read her thoughts and know her dreams. The walls around her upper bunk were graffitied with boys' names she'd written in elaborate lettering with Magic Marker.

I went back downstairs, and Nick came down a few minutes later, a truck in each hand.

Kate gave Nick a tighter hug than I was comfortable with, and he rolled his eyes at me over her shoulder. "And what are you going to do with your life, young man?" she asked him.

"I want to take care of animals," Nick said solemnly.

"So you want to be a veterinarian, huh?" said Kate.

"No, I just want to take care of animals."

Nick had been saying this for a while. He was always bringing home stray turtles and wounded birds.

"It's almost February. I would like to stay the month of February," Kate said formally, as if she were applying for a job.

"February's the shortest month of the year," said Nick.

Kate smiled, as if it was settled. "Thanks for letting me stay," she said, and then she winked at Nick. "I'll try not to make a mess of it."

The next morning at breakfast, Nick was slurping his Cheerios when Kate said, "I don't believe men should have gone to the moon."

Nick gave her a bewildered look. "I want to go to the moon," he said.

"Nobody else should go to the moon," said Kate.

"I believe in astronauts," said Nick.

"I feel like an astronaut's wife," said Kate.

"You're not married," said Nick wisely.

"It's more a spiritual thing, Nick," said Kate, pointing her fork at him.

"You shouldn't point with your fork," he said.

Later, while I was washing the dishes and didn't know where Kate was, Nick came into the kitchen and pulled on my sleeve. "I have one," he said, pointing down at the front of his corduroy trousers. "I have an invitation."

I looked where he was pointing. "The word is erection," I said, "and it's a private thing."

"What makes it go up?"

"What do you mean?"

"It's bigger. What makes it go up?"

I turned back to the sink. A mother must turn to the sink during such discussions with her son. Standing at the sink was like facing Mecca for me. Wiping my hands on a dishcloth, trying to decide what to say, I longed for the days when head lice were my biggest problem. When Nick had caught head lice in kindergarten, I had sprinkled rosemary on his head to mask the smell of the medicinal shampoo, and he had smelled like chicken stew for half the school year.

Kate came into the kitchen then from wherever she had gone and saved me from having to answer Nick's question. In return, I let her watch pro wrestling with Nick when he should have been working on a school project on children's games and sports during colonial times.

Kate was gone when we got up the next morning, and I didn't hear from her for three years.

CHAPTER 15

"It's a fine sermon about fasting
when the preacher just had lunch."

—Ecuadorian Proverb

The next day was Saturday. I still had six weeks to pre-pare for Mrs. Flax's party, but I wanted to make sure I had all the utensils I needed to bake the birthday cake and cookies. After checking what I had and making a list of the things I needed, I stood at the kitchen sink, looking out at what used to be a stand of fragile oaks and weeping willows behind the convent and was now a dense green awning of summer leaves.

I checked my list again, then I took a deep breath, picked up the phone and dialed the number for Colonial Gracious Homes. I held the receiver in one hand and gripped the edge of the sink with the other.

A young woman answered the phone. "Colonial Gracious Homes," she said brightly. "Modern living in the colonial spirit. How may I direct your call?" She definitely did not have a Texas accent.

"Hello," I said, clearing my throat. "Hello," I repeated. "My name is Charlotte Flax. I'm calling about my rent. I live at 4 Harvest Road, the house next to the condominiums."

I'm not sure why I said I was calling about my rent, because, of course, that was not why I was calling at all. There was a brief silence at the other end, and as I stared out the kitchen window I imagined I saw a line of nuns walking through the woods in their long black habits, their rosaries and small prayer books in their hands.

The young woman on the other end of the phone said, "The guard house? May I put you on hold for a moment?"

"Yes," I said, sighing, as I blasted the water on hard and washed an already washed glass.

I stood there like that, with the phone tucked under my ear, washing clean dishes and listening to a Muzak recording of "Greensleeves" until the woman came back on the phone.

"I'm sorry for keeping you waiting," she said. "Are you calling to arrange a tour?"

"No!" I said. "I got a letter that I'm supposed to move, that you need my house, and I love my house. I wrote a letter that was in the *Grove Sentinel*. Did you see it?"

"Oh, yes," she said. "Just a moment, please." She put me on hold for a few seconds, then came back again. "Mr. Winterson is out of the office right now. May I have your number and he'll call you back?"

"Yes, of course," I said. I gave her my number. Then I hung up and watched the mirage of nuns disappear into the woods.

I felt relieved and frightened. At least I wasn't just waiting to be evicted. I gazed at the trees outside the window and thought about my grandparents' pear trees and remembered how my grandmother would set her pies out to cool on the kitchen counter. I preferred that memory to my memory of buying underwear for the undertaker to dress her in for her funeral. All her underwear had been in the laundry when she died, so, while my grandfather was weeping in the basement, I went shopping at the Woolworth's in Minerva, which was having a "2 for the Price of 1" sale on ladies' undergarments. I tried explaining to the clerk that really, really I only needed one pair, but she said it would be the same price either way and made me take two. I ended up wearing the other pair myself to my grandmother's funeral. It was much too large for me, but somehow it comforted me to know that my grandmother and I were wearing identical underwear.

Now I realized that the phone had been ringing for a while, and I finally answered it. "Hello?" I said. "Hello?"

"Hello, Charles Winterson returning Miss Flax's call," the man on the phone said formally, and even if he had not identified himself, I would have known he was from Colonial Gracious Homes. "Is this Miss Flax?" he asked.

Very few people called me that. Most people called me Charlotte, and my students called me Señora Char-

lotte, or Miss Charlotte or Mrs. Charlotte, even the ones
from Asia and Eastern Europe. Even Darius.

"Yes," I said, taking a deep breath. "This is Charlotte Flax. I love my home. I need my home."

"It's a beautiful property," said Mr. Winterson, who
probably was Nick's age and God knows where he lived.
"And, as you know, you are free to stay there until December." He said this politely, sounding pleased with
himself, like he was offering me a little cup of nonfat ice
cream from the new dairy-free dessert store in town.

"Well, thank you for that freedom," I said sarcastical-
ly. Then, after taking another deep breath, "Please, isn't
there anything I can do to convince you to let me stay?"

But Mr. Winterson had already hung up the phone.

I gazed out the kitchen window again, thinking about
Mother Superior and wondering where she was now.
The rumor in town was that she had left religious life
after leaving the convent and had had fat injections in
her forehead to get rid of wrinkles. I didn't know if that
was true. Carrie said she had heard that Mother Superior had gotten married to an ex-priest and moved to the
Bay Area. Wherever she was, I hoped she was happy. I
wondered if she still loved Lou.

I went over to the microwave, opened the door like it
was a treasure chest and took out my father's precious
light blue aerogramme. I wondered if he had received
my invitation to Mrs. Flax's party, and, if so, if he had
read it aloud to his wife and family and maybe even to
his grandchildren in England who all spoke with Eng-

lish accents.

I traced the ten words he had written with my index finger, kissed the paper, then put it back on the microwave's round glass tray and firmly closed the door.

CHAPTER 16

"At home saints never
perform miracles."

—Brazilian Proverb

The next morning, the doorbell rang at six a.m. Nobody ever rang my doorbell in Grove, let alone at six
a.m. on a Sunday morning. People always knocked. In
my half-asleep state, I thought it was Joe ringing the
bell in the bell tower to call the nuns to morning prayer.

I stumbled down the stairs, pulling my bathrobe
around me. I opened the porch door to find not nuns but
Carrie dressed in a purple sweat suit and string sandals.
Her hair was in pigtails with butterfly bows. She was carrying two small thermoses decorated with peace signs.

"I'm worried about you," she said. "I've made some
Chai tea. Can we talk?"

"Of course," I said. "Let's sit out here," and we sat

down on the porch swing like all was right with the world, although nothing was.

"Charlotte Rose, you can go anywhere. Where would you like to go if you could go anywhere?"

"My tai chi teacher in Eugene told me I should go to China. She said I could teach English to the children of iron ore miners in her village." I sipped my Chai tea as we rocked back and forth on the swing.

"Sometimes there are signs from nature when you're going to make a change," said Carrie.

We both looked up at the porch light, and there were moth wings clinging to the bulb.

"Sometimes I think I see signs of what the day will bring when I go out early, while everything is still," Carrie continued, "but all I saw this morning was that the raccoons had chewed through an old rug I'd left by the garbage cans last night." She shrugged. "I'll never get out of this place, but you should."

"I'll send you a postcard, like Mrs. Flax," I said.

"From where?"

I shook my head. I had moved around enough with Mrs. Flax. I didn't want to move anymore, and the idea of visiting a foreign country where I couldn't speak the language frightened me.

"When I was a kid I wanted to be Joan of Arc," I told Carrie. "She wasn't afraid to leave home. Maybe I should get a horse."

Carrie put an arm around me and gave me a squeeze, and we sat that way, hugging and swinging for a while.

"Well, Joan," she said, standing up, "I have herbal tea to sell."

After Carrie left, I did not pack for China, but I did drive to the copy place in town and make a dozen enlarged copies of my letter in the *Grove Sentinel*. Then I walked around town, posting them on the bulletin boards in the Safeway, the laundromat and the drug store when I thought nobody was looking. I even stuck one on the mailbox outside the post office.

I got back in the car and started driving out toward the mall to put up more copies, but as I passed the YMCA, I realized that the last time I had gone swimming was the day Kate arrived. I had my aqua Speedo in the car, so I decided to stop for a swim. I parked the car in the half-empty parking lot. Few people swam inside at the YMCA during the summer, so the pool was usually nice and empty for doing laps.

I swam thirty laps like I was beating up the water, but all I could think about was how much fun Kate and I had had the summer we lived in Tulsa, when we would sit on the bottom of the pool, having pretend tea parties and trying to talk underwater.

As I headed back into the women's locker room, I saw a sign on the door warning that workers were doing emergency repairs on the air conditioning, so women should keep their towels on and change in the bathroom stalls. I tentatively pushed open the door, holding my towel with one hand, but heard only women's voices. I wasn't trying to eavesdrop, but I couldn't help hear one woman complaining that her husband slept with his clothes on, and another crying and saying that her son had dropped out of college to join the Marines. She was crying with relief because he'd failed the physical.

Suddenly, a man's voice shouted, "Men coming through!" and there really were men in the locker room, walking through with their heads down and towels over their heads so they wouldn't see us naked, which gave me a curious thrill.

I dressed quickly, excited by the men's voices, even though they couldn't see me. I brushed my hair, pinched my cheeks and put my damp towel in the laundry basket.

Instead of heading to the mall, I decided that I needed to go back to the library. I drove slowly, steering cautiously into the parking lot. I checked my reflection in the rearview mirror, patted my damp hair, put on a little lipstick and went inside.

The Grove library was quiet, the way libraries are supposed to be. That afternoon, I scanned through some big books on religion, looking for listings of existing convents and monasteries in the United States. There were more than I thought. There was even a Convent of the Sisters of St. Joseph right in Massachusetts, only two hours away.

Jewish women who had had children out of wedlock and had slept with married pediatric cardiologists probably were not high on their list of desirable candidates for religious life, but they wouldn't have to know everything.

—⌂—

CHAPTER 17

"A frog living at the bottom of the well thinks
that the sky is as small as a cooking pot lid."

—Vietnamese Proverb

One hot and dry summer day in Oklahoma, when I was
twelve years old, Mrs. Flax woke me up before dawn
and announced, "Driving is the one thing a woman can
never learn how to do too early. Get up. Get a phone
book."

An hour later she was teaching me to drive, sitting
beside me in the front seat of the blue Buick station wagon while I sat on that phone book, peering through the
steering wheel and driving around a dusty parking lot.

Mrs. Flax always liked to be at the wheel. Men would
look at her while she drove, turning their heads as they
drove by, while Kate and I bounced around in the back
seat. The last time I saw Mrs. Flax, in San Antonio, her

hair and eyebrows and eyelashes were all dyed henna red, and grown men and the younger ones she preferred still stopped on the street to stare at her as she walked by. But when I was fourteen, I was the one who took the pencil-colored school bus to school and back. I didn't get off the bus when it got to my stop. I stayed on the bus as every other kid was dropped off, then crept up to the front to sit behind Joe Peretti, who smelled of garlic and 3-IN-ONE oil.

He drove looking at me in the rearview mirror, as I focused on the back of his lovely neck. Seatbelts and warnings against inappropriate behavior hadn't been invented yet. Nobody gave a damn. We talked and talked and then we talked some more, about music and photography and the purpose of life.

Once, Joe invited me to drive to Amish country with him and take pictures. I do not recall if I even asked Mrs. Flax if I could go. I just told her I would be gone for the day. We did not go in the bus, though. We drove almost three hours in his brown Ford, then spent two hours taking pictures of horses and buggies and eating homemade peach ice cream and licorice, then drove almost three hours back.

During the long drive home, I fell asleep with my head in Joe's lap.

Last night, I looked at a slide of a photo I had taken in Yellowstone National Park, which Nick and I had visited the summer after he turned six. We had agreed we had to go somewhere on vacation, so we had gotten on a train heading east.

The photo was of a geyser spewing in the distance with the fronts of Nick's cowboy boots in the near corner of the frame. I remember that just after I took this picture, Nick looked up at me and said, "Mom, you're gently unmarried."

The summer after Nick turned nine, we took a road trip through the South. He brought scissors and clipped articles from different newspapers in the towns we visited. It was a phase he went through. I drove night and day, day and night, with Nick strapped in the seat beside me or asleep in back, the hot summer breezes on our necks. I have the menu from Jestine's Kitchen in Charleston, where we shared a pecan-fried whiting sandwich, black-eyed peas and fried okra. I have a copy of the complete short stories of Flannery O'Conner, which I bought near her childhood home in Savannah.

On the evening Kate almost drowned, before I went up to the bell tower and she went down to the pond, I sat with her on the porch, getting drunk and dizzy, waiting for my father in the dark. It was a cool night, with the boughs of the pine trees in front of the house dancing in the breeze. I put my arm around Kate and pushed the swing back and forth with my feet, telling her stories about the day she was born. Mrs. Flax had driven off earlier in the blue Buick station wagon, calling to us over her shoulder that "El Señor has returned!" I was convinced she would come back with my father in the front seat beside her, but, of course, she did not, and I never knew if my father was even the El Señor she had driven off to see.

CHAPTER 18

"If you have figs in your knapsack,
everyone will want to be your friend."

—Albanian Proverb

S itting at the kitchen table the next morning, eating
a sweet peach sandwich, I remembered the sheet
of paper Lou Landsky had signed and given to me. I
looked for it in my book bag but couldn't find it, so I
grabbed a red Magic Marker and a legal pad. I carefully
wrote "Save Grove's Historic Home" in bold letters at
the top of the page and left the rest of the long sheet
blank for signatures. I tore off the page and stuffed it in
my book bag.

When I got to class, I announced to my students
that I was being told to leave my beloved home, which
some of them knew from seeing my letter in the *Grove
Sentinel.* It led to a conversation about trying to make

a home in a strange place. I tried to focus the discussion on the difference between being forced to flee your home country and coming to America voluntarily, but nobody wanted to talk about that.

Instead, one young man from Zimbabwe bent his head and said it was too cold in American supermarkets. A young Korean man raised his hand and said, "I want to take an accident course to learn about American habits, like why old people get married." He had to repeat "accident course" three times before I gleaned what he was trying to say. He meant a crash course.

When I opened a folder to hand out copies of a list of idioms, I heard a Dutch woman whisper to another student, "I love vanilla folders."

I was not paying full attention, though. Someone in the room was wearing the same after-shave Lou Landksy used, and smelling it sent me back to when I was fourteen. A Red Sox game always seemed to be playing on the staticky transistor radio Lou kept in his shirt pocket. In the back of the store, there was a wall of white boxes of shoes and a pile of shoes with broken heels that Lou would sit mending while he listened to a game, throwing the bad heels in another stack like orange peels. I confess that I did once imagine lying down naked with Lou. This was on a day when Mrs. Flax wasn't speaking to him, which happened with regularity, and Lou was confiding his love for her to me in the back of the shop so customers wouldn't hear. I was standing so close to him back there. I imagined the two of us lying down on the pile of shoes, the ones that hadn't been fixed yet, with their broken heels digging into my back.

I passed out the lists to my students, and by the time I got back to my desk, the sweet man who had been a dentist in Czechoslovakia and now worked in the cold-cuts section of the supermarket was waving his hand in the air. "I don't understand, Miss Charlotte," he said, "Why do we have to learn these idiots?"

After class, I walked out with some of my students and posted my petition on the bulletin board in the hall. I knew only a few of them would sign it because many were not legal immigrants, but it made them look proud to see me put it up there, and it made me feel good for a moment, too.

When I got home, Kate and Irving still were not there, and I looked at slides again that night to comfort myself.

There were two of Kate and me in our Halloween costumes when we lived in Tulsa. I was dressed as an Indian and Kate was dressed as a cowboy, and I was holding her in front of me with my arms crossed over her chest. We both looked wounded and had a stricken look in our eyes.

Before we moved to Grove, I started thinking that maybe we would stay in Oklahoma long enough for me to graduate high school there. Not that I loved the place, or liked squinting in the sunlight until I thought I'd go blind, or liked the taste of dust when I licked my lips, but we'd lived there longer than anywhere else. Then Mrs. Flax began dating her young married boss, and that usually meant we'd be moving soon. A few weeks later, she came home from work early one afternoon, ran a bath and sat splashing around, hitting the water with her fists. She reached under the bathroom sink for the atlas, opened it at random to the map of Massachusetts and placed a dripping index finger down on Grove. The next day, she dialed information to find a realtor in Grove and was given the phone number for Pine & Timber Realtors, the biggest real estate agency in town, the one that Darius's wife went to work for. Pine & Timber had never dealt with a long-distance client before, but Mrs. Flax charmed the young male agent into telling her about 4 Harvest Road. "I'll take it," she said. "I'll be there in three days."

I ate my way through half a loaf of dill bread slathered in sweet butter clicking back and forth between those two pictures of Kate and me over and over again. Then I got my flashlight and went out onto the porch to pick up the leaflets and flyers that had been piling up, most of them from Colonial Gracious Homes, and throw them into the outside garbage can.

I sat on the porch swing, swinging back and forth like a child, reading the *Grove Sentinel* with a flashlight and thinking of Lou. He had come from a very poor Jewish family in South Dakota. His mother had been so frugal that when his father had died, his mother had cut out and saved the material from the back of the suit his father had worn in the casket because, she'd said, "Where he's going, nobody will see it."

Lou said when he saw his father lying in the coffin he didn't cry. He just worried that his father might be cold with the back of his suit cut out. His mother had sewn a jacket for Lou that included that piece of fabric.

At three a.m. the phone rang. I let it ring twice before answering, and when I answered, nobody was there.

"Who is this, please? Who is this?" I asked. Someone was on the other end, but no one answered, and I didn't have the faintest idea who I wanted it to be.

Then I heard little Irving in the background, shrieking, "Skibbee! I want cars!"

"Please come home," I said into the phone. "Please bring that boy home."

Then the phone went dead.

When Nick was only four years old, he said to me, "Mom, you have to 'sept it. Kate likes things a little dangerous. You just have to 'sept it."

CHAPTER 19

"All ages are
submissive to love."

—Russian Proverb

The next day, I made a special trip to school to see if anyone had signed my petition, but it wasn't on the bulletin board. Instead, I found it in my teacher's mailbox with a note from the Dean of Students informing me that I was not to use the college as a place to promote my own political agenda. I did not know if it was because I thought I might run into Darius or because there were three signatures on the petition, but I felt like I did as a kid when I sat at kitchen tables across America, staring at the gaping hole in a cardboard cereal box where I'd jaggedly cut out a contest entry form or an order form I'd sent in along with cash. I'd sit, eating my cereal, staring through the jagged hole at the bare wax paper bag inside the box, praying for dolls, watches and even toy refrigerators. Here I was, forty-two years old, and I was still waiting.

I decided I had to talk to Lou again. I stuck the note and petition in my book bag and drove to Lou's store to see if he could save my soul.

Lou now had new signs in his window and on the door that read, "Save Grove's History!"

A slight young woman I didn't know was behind the counter, moving her fingers on a wooden abacus like she was doing finger tai chi. She didn't look up when the little bells on the door rang as I came in or when I cleared my throat. When I approached the counter she did glance up for a moment, but her fingers did not stop.

"Is Mr. Landsky here?" I asked.

She shrugged.

I hesitated, and then called out, "Mr. Landsky!" as if I hadn't seen him a few days ago, as if he hadn't slept in our house with my mother, as if Kate and I hadn't slept at his house and heard our mother in his bedroom, giggling into the night and shrieking, "Lou! For God's sakes!"

I called out again, "Mr. Landsky? Are you there?" and Lou came out from the back room with a shoe on one hand, the way he always did when he was polishing.

I walked into his arms and burst into tears. I didn't even look up to see if the young woman at the counter was staring at me.

"Lou," I sniffled. "I need help."

He held me and patted my back. "Now, Shahlotte,"

he said in his heavy Boston accent. "Shahlotte, you Flax women need to all calm down, you hear me? Do you need any extra work? I'd hire you back, you know." He held me at arm's length and looked at me sternly. "And what's your baby sister doing with a little boy? And why does he carry a stick around?"

I pulled away, shaking my head hard. I didn't know why he was offering me work. "Well, thank you, Lou, and thank you for the sign on the door, but I don't want you to lose business."

"I shouldn't do business with those condo people," he said, just as he had before. "I'll boycott, that's what I'll do, Shahlotte. I'll start a work slowdown against Colonial Gracious Homes." He frowned. "Fact is, few of them come in here, anyway. They buy through catalogs or go to the mall." He raised his fist and shook it. "But I'll fight for you, Shahlotte Rose!"

He had a bit of a crazed look in his eye, but I was appreciative.

"Follow me," he said, putting an arm around my shoulder. We went to the back room. "Would you like some vodka, Shahlotte?" Lou asked.

I sat down on a crate of Nike sneakers as Lou poured vodka into two Dixie cups from a bottle he kept on a high shelf.

"Do you remember the night Kate almost drowned?" he said, sitting down across from me and offering me a cup.

I took the cup and drank down half the vodka as if it were medicine.

"I think about it every day," I said. "Why?"

"It wasn't your fault," he said.

I shook my head. "If I hadn't been up in the tower with Joe that night, if I'd been watching her the way I was supposed to, she wouldn't have wandered off. And I shouldn't have let her have anything to drink. She was just a child."

"All that's true," said Lou, sipping his drink slowly. "But if I hadn't been under your mother's spell...."

I didn't know what that had to do with anything.

"That night," I said to Lou, closing my eyes, "I was drunk, and I let my little sister drink." I opened my eyes and looked at him. "I can't believe I did that."

"And I was out with your mother," Lou said, holding my gaze.

That came as a surprise. "You?" I said, staring at him. "I thought she was at some motel with my father."

Lou shook his head. "She was at my house when we got the call from Mother Superior that Kate had fallen in."

After that, Lou and I were both very quiet for a very long time.

"Lou," I said, "Mother Superior was in love with you. Did you know that?"

He shook his head again. "I don't know," he said. "The nuns used to come in for shoes. She was just a young girl when she joined the convent. My marriage wasn't going well, although I didn't know it wasn't going well. But she always smiled at me when she came in."

He sighed. "I have some age on me now."

I surveyed the walls of shoeboxes. I thought about Mother Superior. I believed what I'd heard about her marrying an ex-priest, but I was skeptical about the rumors that she'd had fat injections in her forehead.

"You go through stages," I said. "I don't think your soul changes."

"But look at Carrie," Lou said. "She's changed."

"What about Carrie?" I said.

"She's all yoga and whole grain now," said Lou. "I think she puts yogurt on her face."

"I put sour cream on my face," I said, trying to defend my friend.

"I tell you," said Lou, "she walks around barefoot in the winter."

We were silent again.

"Well, my sister changed from when she was a little girl," I said. "When she stopped swimming, she got wild, and she's been wild ever since."

I longed to be back in Minerva with my grandparents. There were mornings I woke up and went to the chicken coop in my nightgown to get eggs and instead found chicks just emerging from their shells. That meant we'd be selling them. Chicks can go a couple of days without food or water after hatching because they've absorbed their own yolk. My grandparents had a small side business sending chicks through the mail just after they were born. It was a giddy time, packing those noisy little birds and sending them flying around

America through the U.S. Postal Service to families who would do God knows what with them.

Of course, my grandmother didn't call my mother "Mrs. Flax." But she never called her by her name, either. Instead, she'd stand at the sink, stare out the window at her pear trees, shake her head and say, "You never know with children. It's like opening a package of chicks. You never know...."

"Remember that blizzard, and you kids were out in the backyard with spoons, scooping up snow?" Lou said. "And then we put maple syrup on it and made candy? I taught you that. Do you remember?"

"I do," I said. "You shoveled a space in front of your store and put a lawn chair out before you went home that night, and when you came back the next morning, somebody had put a sign on it that said, 'Life Ain't Alphabetical or Chronological.'"

"Well, that's true," said Lou, putting his Dixie cup down on the crate of Nikes.

I had an urgent desire to kiss Lou then, so I carefully set down my cup of vodka and stood up. I left Lou's store without any new shoes to wear to Mrs. Flax's party, but on the drive home I decided it was time to call the Convent of the Sisters of Saint Joseph.

CHAPTER 20

"Plant rice when the ground is ready;
pursue women when you feel passion."

—Tibetan Proverb

When I got home, I did not call the Sisters of St. Joseph because Kate's green Honda Civic was in the driveway again. I parked, then rested my forehead on the steering wheel and tried to sort things out. Mrs. Flax had once let slip that my father was sixteen when I was born. If this was correct, and there was no knowing, he would be fifty-eight now, two years younger than Mrs. Flax.

I slowly got out of the car and went inside.

"Kate?" I called, but she didn't answer.

I heard Irving crying and ran into the laundry room. He was trying to climb into the dryer and was stuck with one foot in and one foot on the ground.

I scooped him up, held him close. "Kate!" I yelled,

pressing Irving's head to my chest and covering his other tiny ear with my free hand.

I heard Kate walking slowly down the stairs.

"Hello! I'll be right there!" she called.

She came into the laundry room with a flushed look, like she'd been with a man. One of the buttons on her shirt was unbuttoned.

I held Irving fiercely.

"Where the hell were you?" I sputtered.

"I went to a free 'Make Over Your Mommy Look' makeup demonstration at the mall," she joked, patting her hair.

"No, I mean now," I said. "Irving was climbing into the dryer!"

"Oh." She shrugged, taking Irving from my arms. "Upstairs," she said. "I was upstairs."

"Okay, and where have you been for the last week?"

Kate shrugged again. "I was staying with friends, and I did a shift at the E.R." she said, picking up the stick Irving had dropped and giving me an accusing look. "I didn't want to wear out my welcome."

That night, when Irving was finally asleep and I was sitting on one side of the kitchen table, reading the newspaper, and Kate was on the other side with her foot up, painting her toenails heron blue, she asked casually without looking up, "Why did you move back here, anyway?"

"Well," I stammered. I went over to the sink and looked out the window into the dark night. I thought I could see the moving shadows of deer or maybe some raccoons. I wanted Mother Superior to march right up the porch steps and tell me what to do. "It started because Nick was born with a hole in his heart," I said, "and I couldn't pay the cardiologist. I wanted to start fresh, rethread my life."

"What are you talking about? Is Nick okay?" said Kate, sitting up straight with both feet on the floor. She stood up and walked over to me on her heels, her eyes wide, holding the nail polish brush in the air. "Is he okay? What do you mean, a hole in his heart? Why didn't you tell me?"

"He's fine. And then," I said, shaking my head, "I kept seeing the cardiologist, and he was married."

Kate said, "I can't believe you didn't tell me about Nick. I don't care what you do with men."

"You should keep a better eye on your son," I said.

Kate shrugged, waving the nail polish brush in the air.

That made me so angry that I walked out of the kitchen and stomped up the stairs. Halfway up, I heard Kate yell, "You should talk, Missy! At least I haven't gotten Irving drunk!"

I stopped still. We'd never talked about the night she almost drowned.

"Kate," I said. "Kate!" I shouted, and, to my surprise, she appeared at the foot of the stairs, holding Irving, and followed me up to my bedroom. We sat down on the bed while Irving sat on the floor, waving his stick.

For a moment, neither of us spoke. Then I said,

"Kate, why didn't you call me when you got pregnant?"
She shook her head. "I don't know," she said softly.
"I thought you'd have a fit. And I thought that this guy would actually marry me, or maybe not marry me but leave his wife or something."

"Who was with you when Irving was born?" I whispered.

"I went to the E.R.," Kate said. She shrugged.

"Next time, call me," I said. "Okay?"

"Deal," she said. "I'm actually really tired now. I worked a whole shift. Helped deliver a baby."

"I need some air," I said, getting up.

I went outside, got in my car and headed to the mall, driving very slowly.

I parked like I was drunk and sat in the car for a few moments, crying. Then I wiped my eyes, checked myself in the rearview mirror and headed into the mall. I had a list of things I needed to get for the party.

I wrestled a big box with an air bed for the twins into my shopping cart and fought off tears as I picked out Barbie sheets for them. It was going to be a full house if everyone showed up, with Mrs. Flax in my room, Kate and Irving and me in the other bedroom, Nick and Regina on the fold-out couch and the twins on the air mattress on the living room floor, but I refused to have my son and granddaughters stay in a hotel.

When I got home, Kate and Irving were sound asleep, so I shut their door and went into the kitchen and cleaned out the refrigerator.

The night Kate almost drowned, after all the screaming and the nuns and the policemen, when she was taken
to the hospital, I was left alone, shaking in the woods.
When I got back to the house, with throw up on Mrs.
Flax's polka dot-dress that I had worn to look grown
up and makeup dripping down my face that I'd stolen
from her makeup table and applied in the bathroom
with Kate sitting on the edge of the tub, watching, I was
frightened I had killed my little sister. I was also frightened that I'd be sent to some kind of home for juvenile
delinquents for being found half-naked in the bell tower
with Joe Peretti and that I'd have to wear a faded gray
jumper and sleep in a cold dormitory with hoody girls
who carried switchblades in their knee socks.

CHAPTER 21

"Affairs of the home should not be
discussed in the public square."

—Kenyan Proverb

The last days of the summer of 1991 were hot as the tropics, and along with a heavy rain, the sound of a deer on the porch woke me at four a.m. one morning the week before the party. I stood in front of the television in my robe, watching a "Dick Van Dyke Show" rerun with the sound off, practicing my tai chi moves—Rocking Motion, Daughter on the Mountaintop, Passing Clouds. Rob and Laura were arguing about something, but I didn't know what.

I went into the kitchen for a cup of tea and suddenly felt an overwhelming desire to walk around the convent grounds, or what used to be the convent grounds. I rummaged in the closet for an umbrella and found one splayed like giant bat wings on the floor. I rummaged some more and came up with an old pair of galoshes in a style the nuns themselves might have worn and pulled them on.

I opened the kitchen door as quietly as I could and then stepped into the dark, rainy yard. I was on the lookout for deer. Joe used to hang a sock filled with human hair on the fence to scare the deer away from his tomato plants, and I once stole the sock and put it under my pillow, praying for my salvation and praying it was Joe's own hair.

I walked down a road that used to be a convent path and was now lined on both sides with condominiums. I wanted to go back—back to the serenity of the convent, back to the little red metal cross on Mother Superior's mailbox, back to eating butter cookies from the blue tin on her kitchen table, back to the sound of Joe ringing the bell in the tower, back to spying on the nuns playing basketball, jumping in their high-top, black sneakers. The very first time I saw the nuns, they were playing horseshoes. A bunch of them were standing in a crooked black line on the lawn, laughing as each one threw a horseshoe into the air and missed the stake. Rusty horseshoes landed all over the grass.

I wanted to go back to the quiet and smell of incense in the chapel, but there was a rec center in its place now. Through the rain, I could see the blinking red lights of all the security systems protecting the cable equipment in the tower. And there was the pond.

I stood by the water's edge for a moment. Then I

pulled off my robe and boots and jumped in naked.

I swam for one length through the cool, black water, pulling through the leaves. I swam hard, racing with myself. Then I turned and swam back, and I could feel Kate's child body racing by my side. I climbed out and shook myself off in the dark. I pulled my robe on over my wet body, stepped into my galoshes, picked up my umbrella and then continued my walk through the Colonial Gracious Homes estate, with all the gray paneled wood treated to look "colonial."

I walked and walked, past the buildings and into the woods as the rain fell across my path in a windblown curtain, and again I saw a mirage of nuns walking in the distance in their black habits and shiny black shoes, their heads bent over their prayer books.

I sensed that somebody was in the woods with me. It wasn't a frightening feeling. I was not concerned. And then coming toward me, I saw a deer, perhaps the one that had been on our porch a few hours earlier. It occurred to me that maybe I was having a religious awakening. Perhaps this was the "tip of the icing," as one of my students had said recently.

I soldiered home, snuck inside and tiptoed upstairs to the bathroom. I turned the hot water on full blast in the bathtub and looked at the calendar of wild flowers I had tacked to the wall. It was Wednesday, August 28. There were only five days until Mrs. Flax's party.

At 8 a.m., as I was changing into dry clothes, I heard Irving begin to cry, but as much as I wanted to go to him, I decided to let Kate care for her son. Instead, I crept back downstairs and out to the car and drove to a mall two towns away, where I hoped I wouldn't see anybody I knew from Grove.

I parked in the endless parking lot, checked myself in the rearview mirror and removed a wet leaf that was still tangled in my hair. I patted my hair, pinched my cheeks, smoothed my clothes and then entered the gigantic drugstore.

Inside the store, I wandered the aisles, basket in hand, searching for the key to long life, or at least a more beautiful life, filling my basket with tubes of anti-wrinkle cream that was supposed to "magically plump the lines" in my face in ten days and other potions that promised to erase the years and restore my youthful beauty.

I stood at the checkout counter behind a long line of women with wriggling children in their carts. I closed my eyes for a moment, and I was back in third grade in Fairweather, California. It was 1958, and I was sitting alone in the cafeteria, as I always did during the first few weeks in another new school. The boys were having a food fight and stuffing Bing cherries into their empty milk cartons, then closing them up and putting them back in the stack of milk cartons on ice, hoping to trick kids into taking them. I had been watching these proceedings carefully, but I did not want the boys to see that I had been observing them. So every now and then, I switched my focus to a mural painted on the cafeteria wall of Pilgrims and Indians celebrating the first Thanksgiving. The figures were big and blocky—large gray buckles on awkward-looking black shoes, feathers that looked like fence posts and some kind of animal that looked like a small camel.

In the lower right corner of the mural, printed in shaky yellow letters, were the words "Painted by the Students of Miss Bannon's Second Grade Class, 1920." Reading those words at that moment in the cafeteria, I was stunned to think that the children who had painted that mural were all grown up now and maybe even married, and maybe some of them were even dead.

I opened my eyes and thought of those gone-away children as I watched the children in the shopping carts in the drugstore checkout line. For some reason, it made me desperately homesick for 4 Harvest Road, so after I paid, I hugged my bag of purchases to my chest and hurried to the car, then headed directly back to Grove.

When I got home, I found a flyer labeled "Beauty for the Maturing Woman" on the front porch. I reached in the mailbox and found bills and another postcard from Mrs. Flax with a photo of a gas station shaped like an Indian tipi. *I dressed up as a Confederate re-enactor!* she had written on the back. *It's almost party time!*

It had stopped raining by then, so I decided to sit out on the porch swing for a while before I went inside. I once dated a man who liked airplane takeoffs and landings, so when he flew, he booked flights with as many connections as possible, but I was not that kind of person.

I sat on the porch, cradling my bag. When Nick was little, he loved cars so much that all I had to do was say, "Want to eat dinner in the car?" and he'd race down the porch steps in Eugene on his little legs and run around to the driver's side, waiting for me to open the door and let him climb in behind the wheel, just as Kate and I had let Irving do. He'd sit playing with the steering wheel while I sat in the passenger seat, carefully sorting around in a bowl of alphabet soup for the letters of his name.

I sat on the porch swing, gazing at my car, hugging my bag of potions, missing my son. And then I stood up, picked up the flyer and went inside.

There was a note on the kitchen table:

Gone with Irving for a few days.

Be back soon.

Love, Kate

Propped up next to the note, against the sugar bowl, was a photo Kate had found somewhere of the two of us as kids in South Dakota, squinting into the sunlight, sitting on the open tailgate of Mrs. Flax's station wagon. Kate was still intent on being an Olympic swimmer then, and we were standing so close to each other, pressed together, our arms flung around each other, that we almost looked like Siamese twins.

—🏠—

CHAPTER 22

"A blind person who sees is better than
a seeing person who is blind."

—Iranian Proverb

I t was the day of reckoning—Monday, September 2,
the day of Mrs. Flax's sixtieth birthday party. She had
called a few days earlier from somewhere on the road
to say she was on her way and definitely coming, but, as
usual, I had no idea when her precise or even estimated
time of arrival would be.

Although the days were still hot, the nights were
cooling down, and, outside, a few leaves were beginning
to turn red and yellow. The tourists from New York City
with their expensive sweaters would be coming up soon
to drive in slow motion along the curvy roads, gazing out
their car windows like they were on a ride at Disneyland.

I had been up baking since before dawn. First I made

tray after tray of chewy chocolate chip cookies, and then the chocolate cake with orange buttercream frosting, which I'd only made once before, for Nick's sixteenth birthday in Oregon.

When the cake was finally in the oven, I grated orange peel for the frosting. Then I went upstairs and tried on different dresses for the party. I had ended up not buying a new dress, and now nothing I tried on seemed right. Various frocks littered the bedroom floor. I stood naked staring at my breasts in the mirror, trying to decide what to wear, then finally settled on my "lots of buttons" green dress. Nick would like that.

Through my bedroom window, I heard geese honking in the distance. They were already flying south. I lay back down on my bed in my "lots of buttons" dress. The honking suddenly sounded like a baby crying, but when I walked into Kate's bedroom, where I would also be sleeping after Mrs. Flax arrived, neither Kate nor Irving was there.

I went back to my room, which would soon be Mrs. Flax's room, changed the sheets, made the bed and put on jeans and a shirt. I did not put on a bra. I loved not wearing a bra. I opened all the curtains and windows to let in the fresh air and bright light of the clear, early September day, the kind of blue-sky day we often had in New England in the late summer and fall, just like in the glossy brochures for Colonial Gracious Homes. The sun was shining, and a slight breeze was stirring the leaves on the sugar maple and copper beech trees.

I checked both bedrooms, fluffing pillows and shaking out blankets like I was the matron of a boarding house. I imagined I could hear the soft weeping of parents who had slept in these rooms after bringing their daughters to the convent, to a life of celibacy and muslin underwear.

The timer in the kitchen went off, so I ran downstairs and took the cake out of the oven and made myself a cup of coffee. I was feeling jittery about the party, wondering if Our Father Who Art in Heaven would show up. He hadn't responded to my letter. I took my coffee out to the porch and tried to calm myself by swinging on the porch swing, but I could not sit still. I leaped up, returned to the kitchen and set my cup on the counter. I pulled up the area rugs in the halls and bedrooms, dragged them onto the porch, threw them over the railing and started beating them as if I were in some kind of movie about life on the prairie. I went back inside, got the mop and bucket from the laundry room, filled the bucket with hot water and added vinegar and fresh lemon juice. Then I took off all my clothes again and dropped them on a kitchen chair. I got my nun galoshes, stepped into them, grabbed the mop and bucket and scrubbed every floor in the house like there was no tomorrow. Then I put my clothes back on and began frosting the cake. Carrie had persuaded the caterer, Celeste, to add the "Happy Birthday Mrs. Flax" at Cooks later.

As I dipped the spatula in the frosting, I remembered Nick coming up behind me once as I was stirring something on the stove in Eugene. He must have been seven years old, and he declared, "If you like a girl and you can talk to her, then she's your friend. But if you're scared of her, then you like-like her, and you can't talk to like-like girls."

"Is that true?" I asked. "The people you like-like you can't talk to?"

Nick thought for a moment, then ran up to his room.

As I frosted Mrs. Flax's birthday cake, I wondered which one I was, a like-like girl or someone you could talk to, and whether I was destined to sleep alone diagonally in my bed the rest of my life.

The party was scheduled to begin at seven p.m. Nick and his older-woman wife and the twins would be arriving from Rochester at around six. Seeing Nick would make everything all right.

I spent all day cleaning, then showered and put on a fresh pair of jeans and one of my grandfather's old cotton shirts. I washed all the dirty sheets and towels and made up the air bed with the Barbie sheets for the twins. I got down an old 300-piece puzzle of the Eiffel Tower that Nick and I had put together one rainy winter weekend in Eugene and counted up the pieces to make sure they were all there. The girls were still too young for it, of course, but I thought I could give it to Nick to give to them when they were older. I opened the fold-out couch and made it up with fresh sheets for Nick and Regina. I even collected a bouquet of wild grasses and flowers to put in my bedroom, where Mrs. Flax would sleep.

At three p.m., Kate pulled into the driveway, beeped

the horn and waved her flirty wave, the way Mrs. Flax used to do. I hurried out to the porch, ran down the steps and reached the car just as Kate lifted Irving out of the back seat and turned to hand him to me like a bag of groceries. I took Irving in my arms, and he said, "More cars. More cars."

"Where the hell have you been?" I asked Kate.

"I helped set a broken leg, and there was a woman who'd put a small cucumber up her vagina."

I just shook my head and carried Irving inside. As I was walking with him into the kitchen, I heard another car drive up. I stood very still, like I was playing a game of freeze tag the way Kate and I, and then Nick and I, used to play. I opened my eyes wide as if that would help me hear better.

At first I wasn't sure, but then I was certain I heard Mrs. Flax's laugh. And then I heard Kate's laugh. They were laughing and shrieking like old high school friends who hadn't seen each other in years, and I suddenly realized I didn't know when they had last seen each other. I hadn't asked Kate, and she hadn't brought it up.

I went into the bathroom, ran a comb through my hair and pinched my cheeks, then walked out onto the porch just as Mrs. Flax emerged from a pink Mustang in a bright purple sundress. Her curly hair was darker than it had been the last time I saw her, but she still looked like a movie star.

Irving ran out onto the porch after me, tripped and fell flat on his belly. I picked him up and brushed him off as Mrs. Flax pulled a giant makeup case on wheels from the trunk of her car.

"Oh, Charlotte," she said, turning toward me. "Come help me with this bag, honey." Then she noticed Irving. "Now, who is this handsome little man?" she asked.

Irving pointed to the pink car and began squirming in my arms. Before I could put him down and go help Mrs. Flax, she was coming toward me, dragging her makeup case and banging it up the steps.

"Now that's an interesting look," she said, pausing in front of me to survey my jeans and old shirt. "Your hair could use some shape. You have a man yet?" She looked around at the house, the porch and the trees as I carried Irving down the steps and got him settled in behind the steering wheel of her car. "I cannot believe you moved back to this place," she said, disappearing into the house.

Mrs. Flax left her case in the living room and headed to the kitchen. Kate and I followed as Irving sat in the car, beeping the horn.

"Now where did that child come from?" Mrs. Flax asked, dropping into a chair and looking from me to Kate and back at me. "God in Heaven, Charlotte Rose, that one's not yours, is he?"

"He's my son," said Kate. "His name's Irving."

"Daddy!" Mrs. Flax shrieked. She jumped up and hugged Kate hard. "Well, that makes me a monkey's uncle!" she said and slapped herself on the ass.

It actually made her a grandmother again, in addition

to being a great-grandmother to Nick's kids. But I knew better than to point that out to her, and so did Kate.

Not knowing what else to say or do, I began furiously scouring the already clean kitchen counter.

"Why you're back in this house, God knows, Charlotte Rose," Mrs. Flax sighed. "Look, there's a whole big world out there," she said, waving her arms and fluttering her red fingernails.

I looked around the kitchen and shrugged. "I've set up one of the bedrooms for you," I said.

Mrs. Flax shook her head and waved off my invitation. "I made a reservation at Cooks," she said, smiling and winking. "More possibilities, if you know what I mean."

Kate and I looked at each other, waiting to see if either of us would mention that I had invited Our Father Who Art in Heaven to the party and that I had made a reservation at Cooks for him, too, although I had no idea if he was coming, not having heard anything from him since I received his blue aerogramme. Neither Kate nor I said a word.

"Well, how do I look, girls?" said Mrs. Flax, twirling around in the middle of the kitchen.

"You look great," we said in unison, as we always did.

In fact, she did look great, the way she always did. Great skin and all dolled up.

Then Mrs. Flax began walking nervously around the kitchen, opening and closing cabinets, picking things up and putting them down. I didn't know what she was thinking. I rarely did. She randomly pressed the button to open the door of the microwave. And there was the light blue aerogramme sitting inside, like an offering.

"What the hell is this?" Mrs. Flax said, turning around with the envelope in her hand. "Is that your new mailbox?"

"Nothing," I said, trying to sound casual. "Nothing. Just a letter from someone." I reached to take it, but Mrs. Flax snatched it away, gave me a suspicious look, opened the envelope and read the letter. And if anyone has ever really turned pale reading something, that's what she did.

"When did you get this?" she asked quietly.

"This summer," I said. "Have you heard from him?"

Mrs. Flax was silent for what seemed like a full minute but probably was not because she was never quiet for more than a few seconds.

"Not in a long time," she said finally. She put the aerogramme back in the microwave and shook her head. "He was something else," she said. "Something else."

I can't be sure. I did not collect evidence in a test tube. But I believe I saw tears in Mrs. Flax's eyes.

I went to the sink and began re-washing some clean dishes, and Mrs. Flax and Kate went off somewhere with Irving.

A little while after they left, the phone rang. It was my Nick.

"Mom, I'm really sorry," he said. "I feel terrible, but we won't be able to make it. Everybody has chicken pox. Becky woke up with it, and Lisa has just started scratching and now Regina has a fever. I called the doctor, and he said it's pretty serious for a grown-up to have it. I'm really sorry."

"I am, too, honey," I said in a monotone, looking out the kitchen window at the mix of still-green and just-beginning-to-turn leaves. "I understand," I said. "Remember when you had them?"

"I took my shirt off and scratched my back on that little chair," said Nick.

"At least you won't get them again." I said, my voice wavering.

"Will you tell Grandma and Aunt Kate I'm sorry and we'll see them another time?"

"Of course, honey," I said, turning on the water hard so he would not hear me crying. As I stared out the window I could have sworn I saw him flying among the trees in those hang-gliding wings. "We'll all see each other soon," I said. "We will."

—⌂—

CHAPTER 23

"The boat of affection
ascends mountains."

—Bengali Proverb

The banquet room at Cooks Inn was decorated with artificial orange maple taped on the walls in an attempt to create a cozy, autumn mood, and there was a fire in the fireplace that looked almost real but was electric. It had the feel of Thanksgiving three months early, but Carrie had arranged everything, so I could not complain. There was a rolling bar in one corner and two long tables against a wall where the food would be set out. There was a smaller table in another corner with a boom box and a stack of tapes on it, and three round tables in the middle of the room covered with orange tablecloths. Each of the round tables had a big orange Buddha as a centerpiece. "Orange is the new blue," Car-

rie had said. The tables looked lost in the big room, but
Carrie had insisted that three tables were all we needed.
"Most people will stand," she had said, "but we'll have
some chairs in case Mrs. Flax wants to sit down and actually eat a meal." We both knew that was unlikely, but
you could never be sure of anything with Mrs. Flax.

There were more than enough chairs for everybody
I had invited scattered around and two high chairs set
up for the twins with two purple bibs with "Little Cooks"
printed on them in black script. I had planned for a total of
eleven people. Aside from Mrs. Flax, obviously, there was
supposed to be Lou, Nick and Regina and the twins, me,
Kate, Carrie and her husband, Tim, and maybe by some
miracle my father. The addition of Irving made twelve,
but now that Nick and Regina and the girls weren't coming, I was down to eight. When I had called Carrie, crying, to tell her the news, she had asked if she could invite
some people, and I had said yes. "I don't know if they'll
come," she said, "but what the hell."

I was rearranging the wineglasses at the bar when
Lou walked in, the first to arrive, in a suit that was too
short and showed off his argyle socks and extremely
shiny shoes. He was grinning like a nervous teenager,
his eyes darting around, looking for Mrs. Flax.

"Hi, Shahlotte," he said, giving me a squeeze. "Is the
birthday girl here yet?"

Two high school students wearing black aprons
with the slogan, "Cooks Does It Better" in big purple
letters, which didn't seem particularly appropriate or

grammatical to me, were pouring ice water into plastic pitchers. Another young man in an apron put a tape of Beatles tunes in the boom box. The other two waiters went over and said something to him, and he shrugged and switched to a tape of New Age instrumental music, which Carrie had no doubt provided. She hadn't arrived yet, though, which I was getting annoyed about. It was almost seven o'clock, and Carrie had promised she would be there early.

Then, on a waft that was as much memory as reality, I smelled Mrs. Flax's perfume, a strong Lily of the Valley scent that on her smelled dangerous. A moment later, she was in the doorway, wearing one of her famed polka-dot dresses and trademark six-inch patent leather stilettos. Lou moved toward her in what seemed to be slow motion, crossing the floor as smoothly as he could manage, holding his glass of white wine high in the air as if in a toast, but just as he got to her, he stumbled and spilled his wine on the skirt of her dress.

Mrs. Flax shrieked and threw her arms around him. "Lou, you're a son of a gun!" The party had begun.

The young waiter who'd put on the New Age music changed the tape again, and "If You Wanna Be Happy" began playing on the sound system. I sang along to the lyrics about never making a pretty woman your wife, but I changed "pretty" to "older." I missed my son so much that I found myself thinking that maybe his older-woman wife had gotten chicken pox on purpose, or was even pretending. I was feeling unmoored, like I could drift into the walls.

Kate finally showed up in a tight, red dress and black spike high heels and immediately handed Irving to me. He was wearing navy blue overalls, a bright yellow shirt and a little blue, clip-on bow tie, and he was clutching another beloved stick. As soon as I picked him up, he pulled off the bow tie and hurled it to the floor.

"It's hard to have a life and a child," Kate announced, heading for the bar.

I loved Irving, but I really did not want to watch him the entire evening, so I walked over to Lou, who was standing beside Mrs. Flax, and asked him to hold Irving for a while.

"Sure, Shahlotte," Lou said. He put down his wine glass and grabbed Irving like a pro, stick and all. He tickled Irving's belly, and Irving shrieked with delight, and Mrs. Flax let out a loud laugh and said, "Oh, Lou! For God's sakes!"

Suddenly Carrie's husband, Tim, appeared in the doorway with a small group of people I hadn't invited but was glad to see anyway, people Carrie had invited. There was Lenore, my sometimes swimming partner, looking terrific in a beige linen suit and matching shoes. There was Dee, without her skis on wheels, wearing a gray sweatsuit that looked a little stained. Then there was a dashing-looking man in uniform standing next to Tim, and it took me several moments to realize it was Tim and Carrie's son, Kenneth, back from Kuwait, saluting at the door. Kenneth looked completely different and quite normal in his uniform, and then I figured out what was different. No glasses. He must have been wearing contact lenses. Anxious as I was feeling, I smiled at Kenneth. I was so relieved that he was alive. He took off his cap and came right over to me. He saluted, clicked his heels and said, "Charlotte Flax, congratulations to your mother on this day."

"Why, thank you, Kenneth," I said. "I'm glad you're here. Are you home for good? Your mother didn't tell me."

"Have to go back Wednesday. My unit is doing security. I'm a surprise," he said, and he saluted again, pivoted and returned to his father's side.

Lou had put Irving down, and the young waiters and waitresses were keeping an eye on him and letting him play on the floor with plastic cups.

I was beginning to get seriously upset with Carrie for being so late when she appeared in the doorway in a saffron-colored sari and string sandals, with henna tattoos on the tops of her feet. She hurried over and gave me a hug. "Sorry I'm late," she whispered. "Had to go to the bus station." And then a man appeared in the doorway and stood there quietly with his head bent.

The man looked like he was in fifties. He was attractive, with thick, wavy, white hair and olive skin, and he was wearing a dark suit and moccasins. Kate and Mrs. Flax headed right for him, like bees to honey, just as I realized who it was. The man was Joe Peretti.

My hands fluttered to my mouth like I was in a silent movie, and I suddenly found it difficult to breathe.

Mrs. Flax reached him first. "You look like a professional man," she flirted, apparently not recognizing him, either.

"I work at a VA," he said quietly.

Mrs. Flax's eyes lighted up. "Joe!" she shrieked, throwing her arms around him. "Well, if you ever do surgery you can take anything out of me you want." She let him go, stepped back and turned around, looking for me.

Joe's eyes found me first, and we stared at each other for the first time in twenty-seven years. I wanted to reach out my arms to him, but they remained pinned at my sides. He took a step toward me and stopped, but I couldn't move. Joe waited, then nodded and turned his attention back to Mrs. Flax and Kate, who were soon joined by Carrie, Tim and Kenneth. They all huddled around him, drawing a curtain in front of him like one of those magic tricks I had seen on TV where, when the curtain is opened again, the person is gone and there's a chicken in his place.

Now, more people were arriving, and I saw Kenneth standing to one side of the doorway in full uniform, saluting each person who walked in.

A stout, elderly couple I had never seen before came toward me, holding hands. They looked about eighty years old. They were wearing matching red windbreakers, khaki pants and white walking shoes, and the woman was smiling as if she knew me.

"Hello," I said, smiling back, trying to be polite. I

knew there had been a wedding at Cooks earlier that day, but I figured maybe there was some other event going on in another banquet room—a cocktail party after a conference maybe, Cooks hosted conferences all the time—and this couple had wandered into the wrong room.

The woman put out her hand and said softly, "Charlotte Flax."

I knew the voice. I knew I knew the voice, but I didn't place it until Mrs. Flax rushed over and shrieked, "Why, Mother Superior! You got yourself a husband!" She clutched Mother Superior's shoulder like they were at a bar. "I always knew you had it in you!"

Mrs. Flax laughed and flounced off, and I stood there stunned, as the sound system began booming "The Twist" by Chubby Checker.

I was having trouble breathing again. Mother Superior had once said to me, "Charlotte, if there's ever anything you need to discuss, you can always knock on my door. Never forget that." She was not supposed to be there with a plump man standing beside her, holding her hand. She was supposed to be sitting in the kitchen of her cottage, in her full black habit, making little designs with her finger in the crumbs on the table as I sat across from her eating cookies and the ice creaked in the frozen pond. She was supposed to be telling me about how frightened she had been when she arrived at the convent at age sixteen and how nervous she had been when she took her solemn vows, wearing a white dress to symbolize her marriage to Christ. But this was not happening. Instead, Mother Superior was standing in front of me in khaki pants and a red windbreaker, introducing me to her husband, Phil, and telling me I should call her Grace now, or Mrs. Canfield, and that she and Phil lived outside Albany, where Phil used to have a construction business. And then Kenneth of all people was pulling me by the hand to dance.

"I love the twist," Kenneth said, removing his cap and holding it in one hand as he started to gyrate. "You just move your feet like you're putting out a cigarette. But you shouldn't smoke. You know, in Holland, drivers open their car doors with their right hand when they get out of the car."

"Well, that's interesting, Kenneth," I said, smiling and twisting. I had no idea what he was talking about. All I could think about was Joe.

"It makes sense, you see? The driver has to reach across himself to his left side to open the door with his right hand. That makes him turn to his left and look back to see if a car's coming. It's safer. Next time I get back to the States, I'm going to write a letter to Congress."

I nodded and smiled, twisting away, and then Kenneth was talking loudly in my ear above the music. "You need to get out of this town, Charlotte Flax!" he said. "It will help you! It helped me!"

I nodded again. I wanted to tell Kenneth that I had gotten out of this town but had returned because I liked living here, but then suddenly Mother Superior and her husband were doing the Twist right next to us, which made me feel too uncomfortable to say anything.

Instead, I scanned the room. Lou was dancing with Mrs. Flax, and Kate was chatting up Joe in a corner. I couldn't believe it. I wanted to walk out of the room that moment, but I couldn't. It was Mrs. Flax's birthday, and I had planned this party. And Joe was there.

Mercifully, it was time to eat. I followed the herd to the food tables, which were now laden with food, and let the teenagers in their "Cooks Does It Better" aprons scoop lasagna and salad onto my plate, but I had no appetite. They might as well have been ladling out raw kangaroo meat. I sat down at a table with Kenneth on one side of me and Mrs. Flax on the other. Mother Superior and her husband were having a grand time talking to Mrs. Flax and Lou and drinking and eating up a storm. Kate was dancing with one of the young waiters, and Joe was sitting at another table with his back to me between Carrie and Lenore. I wanted to leave. I couldn't stand being in the same room with Joe and watching him talk to all these other people. But I couldn't leave before everyone sang "Happy Birthday" to Mrs. Flax.

Finally, the waiters and waitresses in their "Cooks Does It Better" aprons entered the room in a small procession, carrying my cake with sixteen lit candles on it. They started singing "Happy Birthday," and we all joined in. They put the cake down on the table in front of Mrs. Flax. I stood and tapped my glass with a fork, and everybody quieted down. I raised my wineglass to Mrs. Flax and said, "There's nobody like you!" Everybody cheered and clapped, and Mrs. Flax smiled and raised her glass to me, then closed her eyes and blew out the candles in a way that looked vaguely obscene. Everybody cheered and clapped again. Then Mrs. Flax went back to flirting with Lou as the waiters took the cake away to begin cutting it.

I followed the cake back to the food table to see if Celeste had decorated it as promised. She had. "Happy Birthday Mrs. Flax" was written on the cake in loopy red frosting letters that were now being cut up, leaving a piece of red frosting on each slice of cake. I took the smallest piece I could find and tasted it, and it immediately reminded me of the last time I'd made the cake, for Nick's sixteenth birthday, and how desperately I missed my son. I looked around for Joe and saw him in the corner, again with his back to me, talking to Kate, who was gazing up at him with big eyes.

People began lining up for cake, and I decided it was a good time to leave. Just as I put my cake plate down on the table, Darius walked in with a bosomy blond woman, both of them dressed up like they were going to a Broadway show in New York City. The woman looked familiar, but I didn't know where I had seen her. Then I remembered. In the family photograph hanging on Darius's living room wall. It was his ex-wife, Liselle. I stopped in my tracks, gave them both a tight smile and watched Kate walk up to them and offer them each a piece of birthday cake, as if this was how normal people behaved. Liselle didn't seem very excited to be there, and I wondered why they had come. Were they back together? Was Darius showing her off? It was clear to me that Darius couldn't keep his eyes or his hands off his ex-wife.

I had to get away. I didn't know where Joe was and I didn't look for him. If I did and he was looking in my direction, I didn't trust myself not to run right over and throw my arms around him. Instead, I looked for Irving, who was standing near the boom box, waving his stick almost in time to the music. I picked him up and moved slowly around the room, keeping my eyes lowered, until I reached the door and could turn and scan the room from there. Kenneth was standing at attention at the entrance. He saluted me, and I saluted him, and then I backed out of the doorway.

I ran into Kate in the hall, returning from the ladies' room. "I'll take Irving home," I said. "The car seat's in your car, right?"

Kate shrugged. "Yeah, sure," she said. "Suit yourself. The car's unlocked."

I headed out to the parking lot in the mild September night, got Irving settled and headed down the long driveway to the main road, counting all the trees tied with yellow ribbons that I saw in my headlights as I drove by. I raced home, or at least drove at a speed that I would consider racing, and then I took Irving in my arms and walked around to the back yard.

I kicked off my shoes, put Irving down, took hold of the top end of the stick he was clutching and led him slowly by his stick through the trees to the convent grounds. I held his hand tightly as we walked around the pond and carried him piggyback as we walked around the condos. I was surprised we weren't stopped by a security guard and told we were trespassing.

Irving was getting heavy, so I put him down again, and we walked to the bell tower. I went around to the side, away from the door and all the security alarms, and pressed my cheek to the stone while Irving scratched around in the dirt at the base of the tower with his stick. We were out there for a long time, until the sprinkler systems came on. And then I picked up Irving and carried him home through the spray, both of us getting wet.

When we got to the house, he was asleep on my chest, and I was exhausted. I sat on the porch swing with Irving in my arms, and he suddenly let out a cry and fell back asleep.

I was still on the porch at around eleven p.m. when two cars pulled up. Lou got out of one and came around to open the door for Mrs. Flax. Joe Peretti was driving car Kate's car. He had brought her home.

"Yoo-hoo!" Mrs. Flax trilled, taking Lou's arm and fluttering her other hand at me. "Mr. Landsky is going to take me back to the shoe store and fix my shoes. Isn't he a dear? They're brand new and they're too tight!" She ran up the steps in her too-tight stilettos, waving her fingers at me again on her way into the house. "I just need to get a few things," she said. She came back out carrying a small overnight case, and then she and Lou got into his car and drove off.

Joe, meanwhile, had helped Kate out of her car and was now standing at the bottom of the porch steps with his arm wrapped tightly around her waist.

"Thanks for taking Irving," Kate mumbled, wobbling in her high heels.

"Your sister needs to get to bed," Joe said.

"I'm sure she does," I snapped.

Joe looked me in the eye for the second time that night. "Charlotte, help me," he said softly. It was the first time I had heard him speak my name in twenty-seven years, and I could barely breathe. This was not the conversation I dreamed of us having if we ever saw each other again.

I stood up, settled Irving on my hip, went down the steps and took Kate's other arm.

Slowly, very slowly, the four of us climbed the steps in a lurching line dance and made our way into the house.

When we got inside, I carefully transferred Irving to Joe. Then I guided Kate up the stairs and into her bedroom and lowered her onto her bed, and Joe got Irving settled on the mattress on the floor.

Kate fell asleep immediately. I took her shoes off, pulled a light blanket over her and tucked her in like she was a child herself, the way I used to do when she was little.

Then I did something else I had not done since she was a little girl. I smoothed her hair and kissed her on the top of her head. I thought I smelled a faint whiff of chlorine as I bent over her, but it was probably from my hair.

When Joe and I got back downstairs, he went directly to the front door. "Thank you, Charlotte," he mumbled, not meeting my eyes. "Carrie and Tim said I could
stay at their place tonight, so...." and he turned and was
out the door.

After Joe left, I got one of my grandfather's old flannel shirts out of the closet and went back out on the
porch. I sat in the swing for a long time in the cool autumn night, sort of the way Kate and I had sat, getting
drunk and dizzy, waiting for Mrs. Flax to come up the
driveway with my father in the car. Except this night
was different for three reasons. First, I was not getting
drunk. Second, I was not wearing Mrs. Flax's high heels
and polka dot-dress. My feet were bare, and I was wearing my green "lots of buttons" dress. And the third reason was, I was not waiting for someone to return. I felt
in my heart that I would never meet the man who was
my father.

CHAPTER 24

"Little by little one walks far."

—Peruvian Proverb

That night I slept on the air bed with Barbie sheets that I'd made up in the living room for the twins. When I woke up, I threw on a summer dress and cardigan and checked on Kate and Irving. Kate was snoring. Irving was awake, smiling and chewing on his stick. I gave him some breakfast, then bathed him in the laundry sink and dressed him in a little white t-shirt and soft green overalls with cement mixers all over them that had once been Nick's.

Holding him on my hip, I deflated the air bed and picked up the Barbie sheets and threw them into a pile in the laundry room. I didn't have the strength to do tai chi. Instead, I made coffee and went out on the porch with Irving and sat with him on the swing.

I was about to go inside to refill my cup when Joe came walking up the driveway, wearing a plaid flannel shirt, corduroy pants and his moccasins. He nodded from halfway down the drive, and I remembered the first time I had spied on him. He had been kneeling in the convent garden with his back to me, tying up his tomato plants, and I had been smitten. I had shut my eyes and prayed, "Dear God, don't let me fall in love and want to do disgusting things." A few minutes later, he had gotten up and gone into a tool shed, and the second he had disappeared, I had missed him. I had wrapped my arms around the nearest tree, pressed my ear to the rough wood and vowed then to wait forever for him.

I tried not to show any emotion as Joe climbed the porch steps.

"Would you like some coffee?" I asked as he sat down next to me on the swing, which squeaked under his weight.

"No, thank you," he said politely, taking Irving's little hand. "I'm trying to cut down."

"Tea?"

"No, I had some earlier. Thank you."

"More trucks," said Irving.

Joe smiled and smoothed Irving's hair. He was as handsome and wonderful as ever, just older.

"Are you okay?" I asked.

He nodded. "Are you?"

I didn't answer.

The swing squeaked again as Joe stood up and

turned to look at the house.

"They're making me leave," I said, throwing my hands in the air. "This place."

"I heard." Joe shook his head. "Guard house. Crazy."

"Do you have kids?" I asked.

"No, no I don't," said Joe.

"Are you married?"

This time Joe did not answer. He just nodded as he opened and closed the screen door.

"Screens need replacing," he said. "And the swing needs oil. I heard you have a son and grandchildren. That's great."

"Did Carrie tell you about the party?" I asked.

Joe nodded. "She calls me from time to time. I wasn't going to miss it."

"I'm sure Kate was glad you came," I snapped. "Although I'm sure she'll be disappointed you're married."

"Charlotte," Joe said in that tone he had used years before when he was trying to calm me down. "This isn't about Kate. And, besides, my wife doesn't live with me."

"Separated?" I said.

Joe sighed. "Actually, maybe I could use some coffee."

I picked up Irving, and we went inside.

I poured Joe a cup of coffee as he stroked the kitchen table.

"Hard to believe you were born under that," I said.

"Everything's hard to believe. You're good with that kid," he said. "No husband?"

"No. That I'm not good at, apparently," I said, refilling my cup. "So, what have you been doing?"

"I'm a caretaker at the VA hospital in Baltimore. That's where I live now." Joe fiddled with his cup. "I was in Vietnam."

That shook me. I couldn't imagine Joe in the midst of war.

Just then, Irving started banging trucks on the floor in the living room, and Kate came down the stairs and into the kitchen, still in her red dress, dragging a blanket like a child. Joe stood up and gave her his chair, and she sat down at the kitchen table without saying anything. She looked terrible, which was rare for her, with smudged eye makeup and rumpled hair. I got up and poured her a cup of coffee.

"Drink this," I said, putting the cup in front of her.

"Thank you," she said quietly. "I don't think I can take care of Irving."

Joe and I looked at each other as if Kate were our troubled daughter.

"I don't think that's an option," I said. "You can't return him like a present."

"I know," said Kate, sipping her coffee and shutting her eyes. "But I'm... you know, unreliable."

"I'll second that," I said, clinking my coffee cup against hers.

"And Nick turned out so well, even if he's with that older lady with chicken pox," Kate said.

It was the first compliment I could remember Kate

ever paying me.

"So tell me about you, Joe," said Kate, turning to Joe, suddenly sounding almost like her old self.

"Well, I give tours at the Babe Ruth Museum in Baltimore. Right near Camden Yards."

Kate and I looked blankly at him.

"That's the new baseball stadium they're building. The tours are at the house where Babe Ruth was born."

"Maybe we should give tours here," Kate said, "where you were born."

Joe looked down and blushed.

"Why don't you guys take Irving?" said Kate, putting down her coffee cup, and then, before either of us could answer, "So I hear you're married, Joe. Who's the lucky lady?"

Joe hesitated. "She's sick, actually."

Kate and I looked at each other. "Sorry," we said at the same time.

"Not cancer or anything," Joe said. "It's..." He looked up at the ceiling. "Her mind. A kind of early Alzheimer's. One morning at breakfast, she looked at me and said, 'May I help you with something, young man?' The next week, she wore her bathrobe to work. She's taken up with some guy at the assisted-living facility. It happens. She doesn't know me. She's a nurse. Was a nurse. We met in the Army."

We were all silent for a while.

"Look," said Kate, standing up, pulling her blanket around her like a messy toga. "I'm going to get changed and leave. I can't take Irving. I really can't. I just can't think about him every minute of the day. It makes me crazy. I just can't."

"Kate," I said. "You can't be serious. He's your son."

"I mean it, Charlotte," she said. "You have to help me."

Just then, Irving wandered into the kitchen with his stick in one hand and the fire truck I'd bought him in the other. "More trucks," he said.

I picked him up.

"Okay," I said. "I'll take him for now. But not forever. I don't even know where I'll be living in a few months."

"Of course not forever," said Kate. "I just need a break." She crossed her arms on the table and put her head down. She lifted her head and looked up at me. "Could we get out of here?" said Kate suddenly.

"What, now?" I said.

"You and me. Joe, could you watch Irving for a little while? Just while Charlotte and I take a walk?"

Joe looked startled and then quietly said, "Sure. Do I need to do anything?"

"Give him sticks," Kate and I said in unison.

"Do you want to change your clothes?" I said to Kate.

"No," she said, pulling her blanket tightly around her. She walked barefoot out the kitchen door, and I followed her. I looked back at Joe, who was already sitting cross-legged on the floor with Irving, lining up trucks and cars in a traffic jam.

Kate and I walked silently, arm in arm, through the woods toward the Colonial Gracious Homes grounds.

When we got to the edge of the woods, almost to the pond, we stopped.

"I'm sorry I let you almost drown," I said.

"Get over it," said Kate. "You know how you used to say, 'I want to stay put long enough to fall down crazy and hear the word of God'? Well, there's another part to that. If you never do anything crazy, God's going to talk to other people."

"Could we sit on the swing for a minute?" I said.

Kate smiled and nodded, and we walked back across the back yard and around to the front of the house, climbed the steps and sat on the porch swing like old times. It squeaked as we sat down and creaked as we rocked, just like it had when we were kids.

"Remember?" I said to Kate at the exact moment that she said, "So, what are you going to do?"

"That about sums it up," I murmured.

"What do you mean?" said Kate. "Oh, I see. You mean, the way we're different. You think past, I think future."

We sat for a while, just rocking.

"I'm not completely like Mrs. Flax, though, you know," said Kate.

"I know," I said. "Even Mrs. Flax isn't completely like Mrs. Flax. I know you two have your own separate memories." We were silent again. Then I took a deep breath. "Just tell me what happened that night. How did you end up in the pond?"

Kate frowned and shrugged.

I put my arm around her and she didn't pull away.

"Well, next time you're having a baby, give me a call, okay?"

Irving hadn't made a sound all the time we were on the porch. It was unusual not to hear him calling for more cars or trucks.

"It's quiet in there," I said, and Kate and I both got up and went inside to see what was going on.

"We're in here!" Joe called from the laundry room as we came in, as if he hadn't moved out of the house decades ago.

Irving was sitting on the top of the dryer, clutching Joe's right index finger with his tiny hand. They were both laughing. God knows what about.

"I'm going now," said Kate, pulling off the blanket and dropping it on the laundry room floor. "I don't know how long I'll be gone."

She walked over and kissed Irving on the top of his head, and then, miracle of miracles, walked over and kissed my cheek.

Fifteen minutes later she was gone, and Joe and I were back at the kitchen table, sipping from mugs of cold coffee, while Irving played on the floor.

"She'll be back," I said. "She always comes back, and she loves this boy." I put our mugs in the sink. "Do you want to see the house?"

"If it's okay," Joe said.

I lifted up Irving and took Joe on a little tour, wandering around the place like it was the Babe Ruth Museum.

"Your light's burned out," he said when we got to the upstairs hall, flipping the wall switch on and off. "Do you have a bulb?"

I went to the linen closet and found a bulb. He pulled a chair from Kate's room and stood on it to reach the ceiling fixture. I stood below him as he unscrewed the fixture and handed it me. He gave me the old bulb and I gave him the new one, like we did this all the time.

"Thank you," I said as he stepped down and put the chair back in Kate's room. "Now, to continue the tour. I'm thinking of putting little ropes across the doorways to keep tourists out," I said as we went into his old bedroom, which was now where I usually slept.

We walked around the room, stroking the bureau and bedposts, the windowsill and doorframes as if we were making love as Irving shouted, "More doors! More doors!"

"Where are you going to go?" Joe asked as we stood on the upstairs landing.

"There's a real convent not too far from here," I said. "Sisters of St. Joseph. I could go there. I think they'd take Zsa Zsa Gabor at this point."

"You're welcome to come down to Baltimore," said Joe, turning to head down the stairs. "I think you'd like it. They always need teachers down there."

Years before, when Mother Superior had opened a suitcase and shown me the clothes she had worn when she had taken her vows, the white dress and veil and shoes, even white gloves that had turned beige with age, she had seemed to me, at that moment, in her full black habit, like a ship in a bottle, unable to get out. That is how I felt now, as I followed Joe down the stairs.

"People are always sending Babe Ruth memorabilia to the museum," Joe said. "You could help with that. You really need to fix the gutter out front."

"I should," I said, neither of us knowing which suggestion I was responding to.

Joe went back through the kitchen and down to the basement. He came up carrying two screens, and I realized he was going to replace the screens in the front screen door.

"Thank you," I murmured.

I packed him two tuna fish sandwiches on dill bread and three chewy chocolate cookies for the long bus trip back to Baltimore and made him a thermos of tea. While I was doing that, he found a can of 3-IN-ONE oil in the basement and went out and oiled the porch swing.

Joe came back inside carrying Irving's car seat. "She left this," he said, putting the car seat down on the kitchen floor. He washed his hands as I rinsed out a few bowls and utensils and put them on the drain board to dry, and as we stood at the kitchen sink, he said, "I'm sorry I didn't have time to fix the gutter."

And then, God strike me down, we made love right there at the kitchen sink. First Joe was behind me, pressed up against me, and then I turned to him and he lifted me onto the sink. Twenty-seven years of waiting passion, like wild people, me covering my mouth so

I wouldn't scream out, not a thought for where Irving might be.

Afterwards, we sobbed in each other's arms. This was the man I loved, this forbidden love. I had to 'sept it, as Nick used to say. Life was a little dangerous.

Afterward, Joe picked up the car seat, I took the lunch bag and thermos, and we went outside to find Irving quietly sitting on the porch, pushing his cement truck around and chewing on his stick. Thank God he showed no sign of having heard us.

Joe walked down the steps with the car seat and carefully installed it in the back seat of my Mazda. I picked up Irving without getting whacked by a truck or a stick and followed Joe to the car. Both of us were flushed, but neither of us said a word.

We got Irving strapped in, and I headed around to the driver's side.

"I can drive," Joe said, and I handed him the keys.

"Thank you," I whispered as we started down the driveway. "Thank you for coming back."

Neither of us spoke during the drive to the bus station, but we sang along to "Born to Run" when it came on the radio.

At the station, we got out and took Irving out of his car seat like we were a family going somewhere together. We sat outside on a wooden bench with initials and hearts carved into it, next to a cigarette machine and a candy machine.

"Do you want some candy?" Joe asked suddenly.

"Sure," I said. "Why not?"

He walked Irving over to the machine, put coins in the slot, helped Irving push the button and came back with a package of M&M's.

We sat there eating candy, waiting for Joe's bus to arrive, while Irving dragged his stick back and forth between us. We talked about the weather, we really did—how hot it had been that summer, even hotter in Baltimore.

The bus pulled up, and I said, "Remember when you were the bus driver?"

Joe smiled.

The bus door opened, and the driver climbed down and stood at the bottom of the steps to check tickets. I took Irving's hand, walked Joe a few steps and watched as he showed the driver his ticket. As he was about to board, he turned and came back and kissed me on the cheek. "Take care of that boy," he said, and I nodded.

And then he put his arms around me and kissed me hard on the mouth and whispered into my hair, "Come live with me soon, very soon."

"I will," I said. "I will."

And then the bus pulled out, and I got Irving back into his car seat and drove very slowly to the mall. We wandered the aisles of several stores. I was in such a daze that I could have bought him a full-size cement mixer and I wouldn't have realized it. I finally headed back to the house, with Irving in the back seat, shouting, "More cars!"

When we arrived home, Mrs. Flax's pink Mustang was still in the driveway, but there was no sign of Mrs. Flax, not even a whiff of her perfume.

CHAPTER 25

"God is closest to those
with broken hearts."

— Jewish Proverb

The next three days passed in a haze. My fall class at the college didn't start until the following week, so there was nothing I had to do. I mostly stayed inside, cleaning the house and tending to Irving. There was no sign of Mrs. Flax, but I figured I knew where she was.

At about eight p.m. on the third night, I heard a car in the driveway. I went outside with Irving to see Lou pull up in his old work van with a painting of a pair of brown-and-white saddle shoes on the side. I didn't know he still had that van. For some reason, I was glad he did.

"Yoo-hoo! Charlotte!" Mrs. Flax called through the open passenger-side window as Lou came around to open her door and help her down. "I got the best shoes!"

she cooed, clutching Lou's arm and extending one foot to show off a new pair of red high heels.

"Lovely," I said. "They look very comfortable."

"We dipped apples in honey for a sweet New Year, just like I did as a kid," Mrs. Flax said, squeezing Lou's arm. "Maybe I should get back to my Jewish roots."

Mrs. Flax pranced up the porch steps. Lou followed her, beaming, and took Irving from my arms. He set Irving down and tried to show him how to hold his stick like a baseball bat, but Irving wouldn't have it.

Mrs. Flax sat down on the swing, and I sat down next to her. She patted the space beside her, inviting Lou to join us, but the swing was really made for two people, so Lou leaned against the railing while Irving strutted around the porch.

"Where's Joe?" Lou asked.

"Baltimore," I said quietly.

Then the phone was ringing. I hoped it was Joe, but I didn't want to talk to him with Mrs. Flax around.

The phone kept ringing.

"Charlotte, for God's sakes!" said Mrs. Flax. "If you don't answer that thing, I'll have a heart attack!"

I shook my head and went inside. But I did not rush to answer the phone. I stood in the kitchen, listening to it ring on the wall. Ten rings. Fifteen rings.

On the front porch, Mrs. Flax began shrieking, and I finally picked up the receiver.

It was not Joe. It was Carrie's husband, Tim. His voice sounded strained. I could hear a woman crying hysterically in the background. Kenneth was dead, Tim said. He had been killed crossing the street in Kuwait that morning, the morning after he got back. That's all they knew so far. Kenneth was dead, and Carrie was hysterical and Tim was really worried about her.

I bolted out onto the porch and down the steps with Mrs. Flax calling, "Where the hell are you going, Charlotte Rose?" but I didn't answer. I ran to my car and for the second time in my life I drove over the speed limit, racing to Carrie's house.

There were no cars in the driveway when I got there, just Tim's truck. The yellow ribbons tied around the birches and maples lining the driveway were blowing in the breeze.

I rang the front doorbell, but there was no answer. I went around back to the kitchen door. There was a note scribbled in messy ink taped to the glass pane:

Gone to DC to talk to the SOBs.

I realized that they couldn't have left more than five minutes before and had an overwhelming urge to catch up with them and follow them to Washington, but I couldn't leave Irving.

I drove back to the house with tears dripping down my face and onto the steering wheel.

Mrs. Flax and Lou were still on the porch swing when I pulled into the driveway. Irving was sitting at their feet, banging his stick. I got out of the car and walked slowly up the steps.

"Kenneth was killed in Kuwait," I whispered, collapsing against the porch rail. "He was crossing the street. That's all they know. They're on their way to Washington."

I watched Irving banging his stick and thought of Kenneth as a boy, standing unblinking in his thick glasses in the corner of the room at the Throwaway School, saluting everyone who walked in and out. I remembered how Carrie went to him and cradled him in her arms when she came to pick him up. "He was such a sweet boy," I whispered, barely able to speak. "And he'd come all that way for the party."

Lou and Mrs. Flax sat in stunned silence. Then Lou bent his head to his chest and started sobbing, and Mrs. Flax took his hand.

We stayed on the porch like that for a long while, and Irving stopped banging his stick and sat quietly, staring up at us.

Finally, Mrs. Flax spoke as Lou continued to weep. "That poor boy," she said softly. "And Carrie. Poor Carrie. How she loved that child."

We were silent again. And then Mrs. Flax said, "Charlotte, dear, would you mind if I stayed with you for a while?"

Lou and I looked at her in surprise.

"It's just that Nick missed the party, and, goodness, I can hardly remember the last time I saw him," she said. "Maybe Nick and his wife and the kids could come down."

I could hardly believe what I was hearing. "That's

possible," I said. "Would you help out with Irving?"

"Give that little guy to me," she said, letting go of Lou's hand and reaching out to Irving, who actually stood up and went to her and let her snuggle him to her breasts for a moment before squirming free.

"We can stay here until they kick us out," Mrs. Flax said, releasing Irving and finding Lou's hand again. "And maybe you should go to Baltimore after that. I'd help you get ready."

"That would be a first," I said.

Mrs. Flax fixed me with a level gaze. "Well, there's a first for everything, Charlotte Rose."

"That's true," I said. "Very true."

"You could always come work in the store if you don't want to go back to teaching," said Lou, wiping his eyes.

"Thanks, Lou," I said. "We'll see."

I bent down and picked up Irving.

"Hey," I said to Lou and Mrs. Flax, "do you want to come inside and see some slides?"

Mrs. Flax made a face as if I'd handed her a glass of milk that had turned. But Lou smiled and said, "That sounds like a great idea, Shahlotte."

He stood up, walked to the front door and held it open. "After you, ladies," he said, with a little bow.

I brought the projector and slides down to the living room, and we stayed up late looking at old slides from Grove. One of Mrs. Flax in her mermaid costume from Halloween. One of Kate sitting in the bathtub, wearing her bathing suit, cap and goggles, her face covered in some green makeup, preparing to swim around the world. And one Lou must have taken of Mrs. Flax, Kate and me, sitting on the hood of Mrs. Flax's old blue Buick station wagon, with Mother Superior in her full black habit standing next to Mrs. Flax.

Irving was asleep on the couch, nestled under Lou's arm. When Lou's eyes began to close, I switched off the projector.

"Wait here," I said and carried Irving up to bed.

When I went back into the living room, Mrs. Flax was poking Lou to wake up. She walked him out to his van. He got in on the driver's side and rolled down the window, and she kissed him on the cheek. He headed down the driveway, and Mrs. Flax came back up the porch steps and sat down on the swing.

I went out and joined her. We rocked for a while, and then Mrs. Flax stood up and turned to me with her hands on her hips.

"What the hell are you waiting for, Charlotte Rose?" Mrs. Flax said. "Let's go look at some more of those slides, for God's sake. I have no idea what the hell you've been doing with your life, and I'd like to know."

I got up, walked to the door and held it open for her, and said quietly as she walked inside, "After you, Mom."

—🏠—

CHAPTER 26

"Patience is bitter,
but it bears sweet fruit."

—Turkish Proverb

or the rest of the summer and start of fall, we lived in this new shape of a family, with Mrs. Flax back in her old bedroom and me and Irving in my room, Joe's old room, the bedroom I had once shared with Kate.

Kate had gone back to Houston and was working at her old E.R. with her friends. She called fairly regularly and said she was sorry she had left so suddenly and that she desperately missed her boy. She did not say "desperately" in a particularly insane way, so I thought there might be hope for her as a mother after all. We talked mostly about Irving, who cried every night for her the first few weeks but seemed to be doing okay during the day. He had begun letting me hand him a piece of string cheese to chew on and would put down his stick for a period of time in favor of the cheese as he chewed. Once, he grabbed a stick of butter while I had the refrigerator open and began gnawing on that.

Carrie and Tim stayed in Washington for two weeks and camped out in front of the White House, protesting the continued U.S. military presence in the Gulf. A story with a photograph of them appeared on the front page of the *Grove Sentinel*, but as Mrs. Flax pointed out, "What in God's name does that help? Kenneth is still gone."

When Carrie and Tim came back, their two older daughters flew home and the family had a simple service for Kenneth. He had been killed in what officials called a "non-combat accident." He had been crossing a street when a military vehicle came around the corner and rolled. Kenneth could have been buried in Arlington Cemetery with honors, but Carrie and Tim would have none of it. Instead, they put his ashes in a Ginkgo tea tin and placed it on the living room mantle.

I visited Carrie every morning for the first few weeks. Each day, we would do tai chi in the backyard, but halfway through she would just stop, drop her head like a rag doll and kick the leaves. "I can't," she would say weakly. "I'm sorry, Charlotte. I can't even get to the grocery store." She had trouble being alone now, so when Tim was working, she often came over to sit on the porch swing with me or Mrs. Flax, just rocking and staring out at the trees. "Thank you for inviting Joe to the party," I said quietly one day, trying to make conversation, but nothing helped.

Then, little by little, Carrie began taking an interest in Irving.

The first time Carrie came over to sit on the swing, Mrs. Flax and I were on the porch with Irving and decided to take him inside. We were worried that seeing him, such a healthy, lively little boy, might be painful for her. And, that first time, Carrie watched Mrs. Flax carry Irving into the house without saying a word. The second time it happened, though, just as Mrs. Flax was scooping up Irving, Carrie said, "No, that's okay, let him stay." And she sat on the swing, rocking, just watching him.

After that, when I went to Carrie's house to do tai chi, she began asking about him. "How's Irving? What's he up to now?"

Irving was becoming interested in everything, except the vacuum cleaner. Every time I tried to vacuum, he started to cry. When he was angry, he would pound his stick on the nearest hard surface and shout, "Mama car! Mama car!" and the only thing that would settle him down was sitting behind the steering wheel in my car. Most of the time, though, he was good at entertaining himself. He could sit on the floor and play with his trucks and cars for long stretches of time, sometimes putting his stick down and using it as a roadblock.

"I could help out with babysitting," Carrie said softly one day as we were drinking tea in her kitchen. "I could watch him once in a while if you or your mom need help."

I squeezed her hand. "Oh, Carrie," I said, "that

would be great."

After that, with Carrie as a backup babysitter, I did begin working in Lou's store again when I wasn't at school. He needed the help, and I needed the extra income. I manned the cash register and quickly got good again at telling customers, "Shoes should feel comfortable right away."

Irving also became quite a regular at Lou's store. Lou converted part of the back room into a play area, and when Irving wasn't parading around the store in a little Red Sox baseball cap while Lou was busy with customers, the two of them would retreat to the back room for baseball practice. Lou had finally gotten Irving to hold his stick like a bat. Now, they were working on swinging, and I was hoping Irving wouldn't start swinging at home and damage everything in sight.

Joe and I began to speak on the phone every night after dinner. I would sit at the kitchen table he had been born under, and we would talk and talk, trying to make up for all the lost years.

He also sent postcards from the Babe Ruth House with pictures of the house or Babe's glove and long messages extolling the new baseball stadium and urging me to come down. Lou said that if I didn't take Joe up on the offer, he would.

October passed in New England the way it's famous for, with the yellow, red and orange leaves lighting up the hills like a carnival. We had our share of hot summer days that God threw down, and a few mornings when we awoke to a sheen of ice on the pond. It was the usual fall mix, Carrie said. But that didn't stop people from saying, "The weather is so strange this year."

During the last week of October, though, the weather did go completely out of control. Mrs. Flax and Lou decided to take a little vacation and visit the Baseball Hall of Fame in Cooperstown, and maybe continue west to Niagara Falls. "It's not that much farther, and it's the perfect time of year," Mrs. Flax said. "We'll only be gone a few days."

They left on a chilly Monday afternoon, and I headed to the mall to look for a Halloween costume for Irving. I didn't see anything I liked, and then I remembered that I had a fireman's costume that Nick had worn when he was little stashed in the back of the closet. It smelled of mothballs, so I threw it in the wash, and it came out like a fuzzy red apple, but Irving still looked cute in it when I tried it on him.

I planned to take Irving to a children's costume party at the YMCA on Thursday, Halloween day, and then let him wear his costume at home and answer the door with me if we got Trick-or-Treaters. I bought bags of miniature Mars Bars and Milky Ways to put in a bowl by the door. Mrs. Flax had once given out little tubes of toothpaste when we were kids, which I had no intention of doing.

By Tuesday evening, though, the weather reports were warning of a major storm heading our way. I bought candles and extra batteries for my flashlight and old transistor radio, but I wasn't too worried. Carrie said these storms usually weren't as bad as the reports said they would be.

But by Wednesday afternoon, the day before Halloween, the winds were so strong that the tree branches were dancing wildly and the porch swing was banging around like it would blow off its hinges and come right through the house. At around four p.m., I was sitting on the couch with Irving, watching a "Happy Days" rerun on television with the sound off and reading him *Green Eggs and Ham* when the power went out. It was still light, so I was able to get the flashlight and candles and rummage for matches and batteries in the kitchen drawer. I put everything out on the counter so I'd be prepared later, when it got dark. I flicked on my transistor radio. At first all I got was static, but then I found an emergency broadcasting station that said we were in the grip of a real Nor'easter, one of the worst to hit in a long time. That meant no Halloween party for Irving. There was no way parents would let their kids out in this storm.

Irving and I slept on the air beds in the downstairs hallway that night, away from the windows. I layered him up in pajamas under his overalls and wore long underwear under my jeans, and then I covered us with blankets and held him close.

The storm eased a little on Halloween day, but it was still raining and blowing. I dressed Irving in his fireman's costume and let him take a little Milky Way out of the bowl, then put it on the kitchen counter, where he couldn't reach it. At six o'clock on Halloween evening, I was starting to light candles in the kitchen when I heard a dripping near the back door. I put a bucket under the leak in the ceiling, wishing Joe were there to fix it, then heard something knocking against the front door. I grabbed a flashlight and went to see what it was.

Miraculously, there was a small group of Trick-or-Treaters standing on the porch in the rain—one child dressed in a sopping-wet suit, wearing a mask of Vice President Dan Quayle's face, and two dripping-wet clowns, or maybe they were elves. Standing behind them were two soaking-wet adults—a beleaguered-looking woman in a poncho carrying a camera, and a smiling man in a trench coat, carrying a briefcase and holding an umbrella over his head.

"Just a minute," I said. I went back to the kitchen, where Irving was sitting on the floor in his fireman's costume, playing with his fire truck. I grabbed the bowl of candy, took Irving by the hand and went back to the front door. The kids grabbed handfuls of miniature candy bars and cooed over Irving, bending over to talk to him and dripping water on his little red fireman's costume. "Happy Halloween," I said, pulling Irving inside and closing the door as they turned to leave.

I went back to the kitchen, and a minute later I heard knocking at the front door again. I went to the door with Irving and the bowl of candy. It was the man in the trench coat without the woman or little kids. He had set down his briefcase and folded his umbrella.

"Hello," he said with a trace of an English accent,

smiling and extending a dripping-wet hand. "My name is Leonard Frank. Are you Mrs. Charlotte Flax?"

"Yes," I said, reaching out to shake his hand. "Yes, I am." His wet hair was gray and curly, but his eyes and eyebrows were dark. I looked into his eyes and saw what I saw when I looked in a mirror into my own eyes—the eyes of a person old and young at the same time. This was not the parent of a Trick-or-Treater standing on my porch during a Halloween storm. This was my father.

The moment I had been waiting for all my life was not at all what I had expected. There were no fireworks. There were no bells ringing perfect chimes. But when I shook his hand, I could see why Mrs. Flax had fallen for him. His grasp was firm and warm, as if he would never let me go. We stayed that way for a moment, holding hands, and I felt strangely comfortable. It was interesting that his name was Leonard. That was the name I had made up for his reservation at Cooks for Mrs. Flax's birthday party, which Carrie had persuaded Cooks not to charge me for when he didn't show up. Had I heard Mrs. Flax use his name when I was a child? But Frank. That name I had never heard. If he and Mrs. Flax had stayed together, I realized, my name would be Charlotte Frank.

I let go of his hand and looked past him to the driveway, but I didn't see a car.

"How did you get here?" I asked, as if I were speaking to someone I had known all my life instead of to a perfect stranger, which he was.

"I took a taxi from the train station," he said. "I forgot it was Halloween. I've been in the U.K. for so long."

Forgot Halloween? How could he forget Halloween? But then I reminded myself that, whatever his handshake felt like, he had not proved to be a reliable man.

We stared at each other as the water from his umbrella formed a puddle on the porch and the swing jerked around in the wind.

"Would you like to come in?" I finally thought to ask.

He hesitated for a moment. "Thank you," he said, stepping inside.

Irving stared up at him as he stood dripping in the dark front hall. "Whobody is it?" Irving asked, reaching for my hand. "Whobody" was his newest word.

"Please, take off your coat. You can hang it up here," I said, pointing to the rack on the wall. He took off his coat, felt around for the peg and hung it up. He looked very fit, like he played soccer or football or whatever they called it in England, and his pants definitely looked like trousers rather than American pants. He smelled of cherry pipe tobacco.

He looked down at his wet feet, then up at me. "Shall I take off my shoes?" he asked.

"No, no need," I stammered. If he had been a normal father visiting me like normal family, I imagined I wouldn't have minded seeing him in wet socks. I might even have offered him a dry pair of old sweat socks. But I was not ready for that. It seemed a bit too intimate.

"The power's out," I said. "I'm sorry. Let's go into the kitchen. I have candles in there, and tea."

He followed me into the kitchen, which actually looked quite welcoming by candlelight, like a little American still life. What a family portrait we would make, I thought: a grandmother with her sister's son and the dripping-wet father she had never met before.

Irving climbed up on a chair and stood at the table as I gave him a green banana to pound with his stick.

My father stood by the table, still holding his briefcase.

"Please, sit down," I said. "I'll make some tea." I heated water on the gas stove, which was still working, and put two cups on the table. "I'm afraid I only have chamomile," I said.

"Chamomile would be lovely," he said with that hint of a British accent.

I put a candle and a loaf of dill bread on the table and sat down across from him. I folded my hands and cleared my throat, which I imagined was the appropriate thing to do when meeting one's father for the first time at age forty-two.

"Why did you write to me..." I hesitated, "...Mr. Frank?" There was so much I wanted to ask, but that seemed like a good place to begin. "What can I do for you?"

He took a pen and some papers out of his briefcase, put them on the table and smiled. "Well, I've developed quite an interest in genealogy over the past few years," he said. "A passion, you might say. I'm hoping to make it my profession. There's a conference in Boston next week that I've been planning to attend since spring. And I realized that if I intend to make genealogy my line of work, I should try to track you down while I was in the States and complete my own family tree."

I stared at Leonard Frank, and Irving started bouncing up and down on his chair, as if he knew how crazy that sounded. This man who didn't care about my existence for forty-two years decided to find me now because he wanted to be a genealogist?

"Track me down?" I blurted. "You care about your family tree, but not about your actual family?"

He looked puzzled, as if he could not comprehend what I'd said. He didn't seem offended, just confused. He shuffled his papers. "I have a chart," he said. "We might be related to the Frank family." He looked up at me. "You know, Anne Frank."

My mouth fell open. "I doubt that very much," I finally managed to say.

"Well, I haven't found a link yet," he said as he pulled a big piece of thick paper from his briefcase and unfolded it on the table. "Is this my grandson?" he asked, nodding to Irving as if he'd just noticed him.

"This child is no relation to you," I said, reaching over to stop Irving from climbing onto the table. "But I have a grown son, Nick, and he has two girls, so you're a great-grandfather now, if you want to put that in."

Mr. Leonard Frank carefully wrote down Nick, Regina and the twins' names on his precious chart. I cannot say I felt anger toward this man as he did this. It was more a sense of bewilderment.

"Are you married?" I asked him as he scrutinized

his chart by candlelight. "Do you have children? Do you have grandchildren? I mean, other children and grand-children? In England?"

He didn't answer. It was as if he hadn't heard me.

And then I said, "My mother is in town if you want to see her. She's out of town now, but she'll be back in a few days."

At that, Mr. Frank looked up, startled. He frowned and shook his head. "No, no, none of that, I'm not good at that, none of it," he said, picking at a piece of candle wax that had melted onto the table. "And I really must get to Boston."

"Where are you staying tonight?" I asked, and Mr. Frank frowned again, as if he hadn't thought that through. He didn't have a car, and he couldn't call a taxi. I knew the answer. My father would be sleeping on my couch.

"You're welcome to stay here," I said.

"You are very kind, Charlotte," he said. "Why does that boy carry a stick?"

I only vaguely heard his question after he spoke my name. I'd lain in bed countless nights for most of my life imagining this moment, but the effect of finally hear-ing my father say my name out loud was different than I'd thought it would be. It was not earth shaking, but I knew it was one of those moments that would divide my life into before and after, like the night my grandmother died, and the night Bill and I made a baby, and the day I gave birth to Nick. In a way, it was all I needed to hear.

I picked up Irving, propped him on my hip and escorted Mr. Frank upstairs and pointed out the bathroom by flashlight. I handed him sheets, a pillow and a blanket and led him back downstairs. He held the flashlight while I lighted a candle, then I left the flashlight with him and took the candle and Irving up to our room.

I did not sleep a wink that night. I couldn't look at slides because the power was out. I thought about whether I would have wanted to show my father slides of my life if I'd had power, but I couldn't say I would have. I did not creep downstairs to see if Mr. Frank was able to sleep, either. Every now and then, a strong wind gust would hit the house, and I imagined that the wind might whip the house off its foundation and we'd have a Wizard of Oz situation, that my house would spin to another state with us along for the ride. But for the first time in as long as I could remember, I actually found myself not thinking about the past.

In the morning, remarkably, all was quiet. The sky was clear, and the storm was over. I got dressed before I went to use the bathroom in case Mr. Frank was up. I did not want him to see me in my bathrobe. I changed Irving and dressed him in a soft t-shirt and fresh overalls and quietly took him downstairs.

Mr. Frank was awake and sitting on the couch, sorting through papers. He did not look particularly rumpled, considering that he'd slept in his clothes, although he needed a shave.

I gave Mr. Frank tea and made him Bisquick pancakes, which he seemed to enjoy.

"Do you do anything besides genealogy?" I asked, sitting across from him as he ate.

"I play saxophone with a small jazz group," he said. "I write some poetry. And I teach English to foreign students at the University of Leeds."

I smiled. "I do something similar," I said. "I teach English to new immigrants."

After breakfast, Mr. Frank said he was going to walk to town and then catch a bus to Boston. He refused my offer to drive him to the station.

I went out on the porch as he gathered his things to see if the paper was there, but it wasn't. Instead, the porch and steps were matted with twigs and wet leaves, the yard was strewn with broken tree branches covered in mud, and the porch swing lay in a heap like a seat from a crashed carousel ride under a tangle of chains that had been yanked out of the porch ceiling by the wind. I breathed in the clean air. There was a hint of a sea breeze.

Mr. Frank followed me out onto the porch and took in the wreckage. He shook his head. Then he put down his briefcase. "Well," he said, extending his hand.

"Well," I said, offering mine. We shook hands, and that was that.

Irving came out, holding his stick, and I lifted him onto my hip as I watched Mr. Frank walk down the steps with his umbrella and briefcase and start picking his way through the debris on the driveway and making his way down to the road. As he reached a bend that would take him out of sight, he turned back, smiled and waved, and I took one last look at my father and waved goodbye.

After he left, I went back inside and put on my nun's galoshes and stuffed Irving's feet into little boots that Lou had brought him from the store. Then Irving and I walked back onto the porch, hand in hand, to see what the storm had wrought. We walked carefully down the slippery steps to the front yard and started picking up fallen branches as if it was a regular day. We worked out there in the messy yard for almost half an hour, and then I stopped and surveyed our raggle-taggle stack of twigs and limbs. Irving was covered in mud and happy as a clam, picking up sticks and throwing them onto the pile.

I brushed my hair from my eyes with a dirty hand, watching Irving move around the yard, and I knew I had to call Kate. I loved this boy, but I could not raise him. I would keep him until I had to pack up and leave Grove. Then I would take him back to Kate in Texas and spend some time with them there.

And then? I wasn't sure. Maybe I would actually go to China to teach English to the miners' children in my tai chi teacher's village. After that, there was a very good chance I would move to Baltimore.

I shook my head. Irving had a good-sized twig in his hand. I picked up a pine cone and tossed it to him. He swung his stick like a baseball bat and, for the first time, made contact and hit the pine cone back.

I laughed and clapped. "Go, Irving!" I shouted.

"Whobody wants cars!" he shouted back.

I looked out over the yard and driveway at the tumbledown remains of the storm as Irving dug through a pile of leaves, and I remembered something a Tibetan student had once said to me.

"Life is a baffle, Irving," I said as he handed me another pine cone. "Life is a baffle on this earth."

Acknowledgments

With great thanks for the kindness and keen eyes of my editor, Gini Kopecky Wallace. Thanks also to my agent, Malaga Baldi, to Bob Lascaro and Charles Salzberg at Greenpoint Press, and to Susan Breen, Lauri Halderman, Michael Hill, Sally Koslow, David Slavin and Carol Weston.

About the Author

Patty Dann is the author of the novels *Mermaids* and *Sweet & Crazy* and the memoirs *Baby Boat: A Memoir of Adoption* and *The Goldfish Went on Vacation: A Memoir of Loss*. Her work has been translated into French, German, Italian, Portuguese, Dutch, Chinese, Korean and Japanese. *Mermaids* was made into a feature film starring Cher, Winona Ryder and Christina Ricci.

CPSIA information can be obtained at www.ICGtesting.com
Printed in the USA
BVOW040123140613

323299BV00001B/5/P